TONY STORY

MEEK MILL

G
STREET CHRONICLES

Published by:

G Street Chronicles
P.O. Box 1822
Jonesboro, GA 30237-1822
www.gstreetchronicles.com
fans@gstreetchronicles.com

Contributing Author: George Sherman Hudson
Executive Editor: Shawna A.

ISBN 13: 978-1-9384427-0-4
ISBN 10: 1938442709
LCCN: 2013931246

Join us on our social networks

Facebook
G Street Chronicles Fan Page
G Street Chronicles CEO Exclusive Readers Group

Follow us on Twitter
@GStreetChronicl

TONY STORY

I dedicate this book to

the streets of Philadelphia

Based on songs Tony Story 1 and 2

FOREWORD

by

CESS SILVERA

Director of the movie, "Shottas"

"Tony killed his man Ty for a whole brick...lined him up and gave him the whole clip." Those are the first words Meek Mill spit on his song Tony Story.

The first time I heard that song I was on a flight from Miami to Los Angeles. Hours earlier, my assistant had downloaded new music to my iPod for my five-hour flight. I had no clue of the treat my ears were in for. Tony Story came on and I recall my finger being stuck on the playback button. I played that song over and over. After the profoundness of it sunk in, I remember subconsciously muttering to myself, "This is some of the realest shit I've heard in a very long time!" I knew then that I was listening to a master at work. Tony Story is an unflawed piece of jewel, a well-crafted portrait of street life by a wordsmith who obviously had sat at the table and faced off with many snakes.

I had listened to Meek's music before that, but I can honestly say on that flight, on that day, that song—Tony Story—made me a Meek Mill fan.

Listen to Meek tell it and you will come to find out that there is a Tony in every hood that litters America's inner cities. To a fortunate few, these places are the wasteland, to many this is home. These are also the breeding grounds where cutthroat ideas are conjured up and carried out daily by people you trust; yes, people you grew up with like Tony, and his mans and them.

Even with his newfound fame, Meek Mill is still sitting at the table, dead smack in the streets of North Philly where he grew up. God knows, Philadelphia or more fondly known as Illadelphia or the City of Brotherly Love, has seen and continues to see more than its share of Tonys. In this book, Meek peels back the mask and reveals what it takes to survive from day to day as a young hustler with ambitions to succeed.

As I have stated the obvious earlier, I jumped at writing the foreword to this book because I am a big fan of Meek Mill's music. Just like Meek, I've had, and continue to have, my fair share of run-ins with Tony. I've met Tony in the gritty streets of Kingston Jamaica, Miami, and in the concrete jungles of Flatbush Brooklyn, places where most of my formative years were shaped and spent. Again, please believe Meek when he said, "There's a Tony in every hood"…as we Jamaicans would say, "Yeah mon, dere is a fuckin' Tony in every blooclaat place." Translation, there is a Tony everywhere.

Tony Story could have been ripped out of any scene in my movie, *Shottas*, because Tony is not only a street hustler or a thug. Tony is also a politician, a cop, an informer or even that pretty bitch you woke up next to this morning. Shit, now that I've spent most of my days negotiating movie deals with Hollywood types, I've met other versions of Tony. Hollywood Tony is fast talking, mostly white, sometimes black, dressed up in expensive designer suits, and dining on Sunset Boulevard puffing on over-sized cigars instead of blunts. That motherfucker Tony has come a long way. He has evolved and continues to do so; and that is what makes Tony so fucking dangerous. That is what makes Meek Mill's words in this book so profound.

This book could easily be described as a street survival

manual that every hustler or aspiring street entrepreneur should keep handy. It could be the difference from ending up like Ty or Paulie.

Through his music, Meek proved over and over his command on the street vernacular. Now a published author, he once again changed the game because he is taking his fans on a literary ride with a story they can definitely relate to. The difference between Meek Mill's book and others is the fact that his is conceived from a gritty and honest place that not too many other scribes have trod or dare to trod. Meek's book has the same unapologetic and confrontational honesty that his music is constructed in. It is his music being placed between pages instead of over a thumping beat. The reader will not be bopping their head, but they will definitely be awe-inspired by street tales marred by violence, deceit and sometimes even love or lack there of.

One of Philly's favorite sons now possesses the power to have his fans not only jam to his music, but read his book that contains a story that they have a stake and interest in.

Meek Mill's Tony Story will not only be widely read on rooftops of Philly's apartment buildings by street hustlers, but with his knack for true storytelling, this book will make it into book clubs everywhere. It will definitely be on the list of die-hard Hip Hop fans, white and black Suburban kids and their curious parents who indulged in the culture from somewhat of a safe distance. The intoxication is inescapable.

I take the liberty to respectfully repeat the question of the late and great Notorious BIG… "Who would think that Hip Hop would take it this far?" Answer: *Meek Mill.*

Acknowledgements

First off I want to thank God. Without Him none of this would be possible.

I would like to thank my mom, my grandmom, and especially my sister Na, for always being there for me, and believing in me when I didn't believe in myself.

To all my aunts, uncles, cousins, and real friends who continue to hold me down, I appreciate y'all; thanks.

To my son Papi—everything I do is for you, I LOVE YOU! My only mission in life is to make you proud.

To those who are instrumental in converting my vision of "Tony Story" into a reality—MMG, DreamChaser Records, Atlantic Records, GSTREETCHRONICLES, and James Lindsay —words cannot express how much I appreciate you, but a special thank you goes to Isaiah (Zay) Williams. "They say in a sleep state the brain thinks more visually and intuitively, as DreamChasers we accomplish that wide awake…" Zay has embodied this statement with showing nothing less than dedication and the determination to breathe life into the characters in this book. For that, I am forever grateful.

Last but not least, I have to thank the City of Philadelphia for being in my corner always and for being the catalyst of events for this book.

To every reader, every reviewer and every fan of this movement, y'all inspire me to LIVE MY DREAMS! Without you, all of this would mean nothing.

TONYSTORY

PROLOGUE

G STREET CHRONICLES
~A NEW URBAN DYNASTY~

WWW.GSTREETCHRONICLES.COM

The mangy black cat scurried across the street from behind the apartment's dumpster where the ski-masked man dressed in all black invaded its spot. The black-clad figure crouched down low, waiting patiently for his prey. The smell of the recently smoked Kush-filled blunt still clung to his clothes.

A few minutes later, a lone man dressed in the latest urban wear and a single gold chain exited the apartment carrying a small leather bag that contained thirty-six thousand dollars. On a mission to buy a brick of some of the best coke on the street, he walked briskly toward his late-model Oldsmobile, which he used strictly for pickups and drop-offs. He had almost reached his car when his cell phone started vibrating in his pocket.

"Yeah," he answered, after looking at the display screen and seeing it was Tony calling. "Okay, Broad and Snyder... A'ight, I'm getting in the car now. I'll be there in twenty minutes," he said, then ended the call.

Thunder boomed and lightening lit up the dry sky as the

masked figure rose slowly like a lion about to pounce on its prey. He used the pitch-black darkness to his advantage as he quickly stepped from behind the dumpster, clutching a long-nose .357 revolver which he dubbed The Cannon. Returning his cell phone to his pocket and fumbling with his keys gave the masked man enough time to creep up on him without being noticed. Just as he hit the button on the key fob and opened the door, fire spit from the .357 pointed at his back.

Boom! Boom!

The first shot penetrated the man's shoulder, while the second almost decapitated him as the hollow point tore through his neck, sending him face forward into the side of his car. The masked man rushed him and snatched the bag from his hand before his body crumbled to the ground, leaving streaks of blood where he fell. The gunman then hurried away from the scene, jumped behind the wheel of the stolen pick-up truck, and was on his way to North Philly to meet Tony.

Tony sat in the vacant furniture store parking lot waiting for Mike to show. With no re-up money and Ty having him on hold, he resorted back to the streets, pushing up on the young robber Mike who was thirsty for a come up. Mike was putting the pistol down around his way, robbing anybody who moved. One evening, Tony propositioned the youngster, convincing him to leave the petty licks alone and get some real money. After running the plan by him, Mike was game. The youngster wanted riches and didn't care who he had to take down to get it.

Minutes later, Tony saw Mike pulling into the lot. He pulled up next to him and killed the truck's lights. Not wasting any time, Tony stepped out of his silver Chrysler 300 and approached the truck.

"Everything good?" Tony asked.

"Homie, shit was sweet as hell, just like you said." Mike smiled and held up the bag of money.

Mike's smile was simultaneous with the gun blast that caught him totally off guard. The youngster clutched his chest like it was on fire. He fought hard to breathe as Tony reached over him through the window and grabbed the bag containing the cash. Although unable to speak, he stared at Tony in disbelief. In his last seconds, he couldn't believe one of the only people he trusted and looked up to had just ended his life.

G STREET CHRONICLES
~A NEW URBAN DYNASTY~

WWW.GSTREETCHRONICLES.COM

TONY STORY

CHAPTER 1

G STREET CHRONICLES
~A NEW URBAN DYNASTY~

WWW.GSTREETCHRONICLES.COM

The sun reflected off the windows of the black S600 Benz sitting on Lexani wheels as it rolled to the intersection of Point Breeze and Dickerson. The driver of the flashy car stopped to make sure he had the right-of-way before pulling off.

Tony and Ty had also stopped at the intersection, waiting for the car to pass. They knew behind the Benz's tinted windows sat Reese, one of the biggest and well-known dealers in this part of South Philly.

"Man, one day we gonna be pushing one of them," Ty said as they continued to ride their bikes down 18th Street to their block, hoping to make a sale along the way.

"Yo, youngblood!" one of the neighborhood fiends called out while slowly jogging down the block to catch up with the boys.

"What up?" Tony asked, hoping for a potential sale.

"Say, lil' bro, hit me with two for these sixteen ones I got. Work wit' a nigga, man," the fiend begged, displaying a mouth full of rotten teeth.

"I got one for ten dollars, man. Two is gonna cost twenty. Ain't no specials over here," Tony replied as he looked at the crumbled old bills the man gripped tightly in his hand.

"I got you man, but just this one time," Ty interjected.

Tony's sideways glance would've spoken volumes if Ty had seen it, but he was too busy digging through his pocket to grab two small baggies of crack from the bundle he carried in a sandwich bag.

"Y'all boys better get y'all butts in here right now!" Mrs. Mae called out from the front porch of her row house.

With both hands on her hips, Ty's mother stood there in a cotton nightgown with rollers in her hair. She didn't care who saw her. When it came to trying to keep those two boys in line, she'd run down the street and around the corner in her night-gown.

Tony and Ty had been raised in South Philly by two single mothers, Mae Daniels and Cathy Thomas. They were like brothers from another mother. Their birthdays were even in the same month. The two were very different from teens their age. Their dreams and aspirations had surpassed those of their peers. At the young age of sixteen, they had some real street dreams. They envisioned themselves riding in the flyest whips, fucking the baddest bitches, and flipping bricks until they had the city on lock.

5 YEARS LATER...

Ty chilled in the passenger seat of his 750 BMW with Bianca behind the wheel as they cruised through Philly. While riding down the different city blocks, he thought about how far he'd come in just over a year. The hard grinding and flipping had finally paid off. The ten bricks he moved a week may have been small to a few, but to most, he was "The Man" in the city.

Today was his mother's birthday, and they had just left King of Prussia Mall where he purchased a diamond pendant necklace and a bouquet of red roses for Mrs. Mae. Ty may have played in the streets hard, but he was still a mama's boy.

Bianca made a left on to Carpenter Street and pulled up in front of his mother's house, the same house where Ty grew up.

"Come on," he told Bianca.

He had grown quite fond of her over the two months they had been seeing each other.

"Oh, I can finally meet Moms, huh?" Bianca was surprised by his invitation for her to go with him since all the other times they had come to his mother's house, he would tell her to wait in the car.

"Yeah, you moving on up," Ty said playfully, as he took the keys from Bianca, grabbed her around her tiny waist and gently kissed her full lips. Then he tapped her on her ass, locked the car, and headed up to the door.

Ty used his key to gain entry. As soon as he stepped inside, the smell of bacon hit him in the nose.

"Yo, Ma! Where's the birthday girl?" Ty called out to his mother, who was in the kitchen cooking a late breakfast.

He led Bianca through the cramped but cozy home to the

kitchen. Mrs. Mae smiled from ear to ear as Ty walked in holding the roses and a small gift box. Bianca stood in the background as Ty embraced his mother.

"Who you calling *girl*, lil' boy?" Mrs. Mae replied lightheartedly as Ty smothered her with a hug and kisses on her forehead.

"Happy birthday Ma." He handed her the roses and the gift wrapped neatly in gold paper.

"Oh. Ma, this is Bianca." Ty made the introduction as Bianca smiled.

"Happy Birthday Mrs. Daniels," she said, speaking in a timid voice.

"Hey, Bianca. Nice to meet you, and please, call me Mae. You're a pretty little somethin'."

"Thank you," Bianca answered and smiled from ear to ear.

Mrs. Mae spoke politely; however, her focus was more on removing the wrapping paper from the little box so she could see what she knew would be something beautiful from her son.

As the lid separated from the box, her eyes opened wide and her mouth fell open.

"Awww! Thank you, baby!" Genuinely excited, tears welled up in her eyes.

Bianca stood by the entrance to the kitchen watching Ty and his mother. She teared up as well, while witnessing how happy Ty had just made his mother. She also saw where he got his good looks. They both had light skin, and pretty, curly hair. Both Mrs. Mae and Ty were average height so his father must not have been real tall either.

Ty had a very close relationship with his mother. When Ty was only three months old, Cecil Daniels, his father, was killed in a car accident. Cecil had been the sole provider of the household, so after his death things got hard for Mrs. Mae. With no life insurance or savings, she was left to fend for herself with their newborn baby. Being a survivor, she did just that. Mrs. Mae managed to survive with low-paying odd jobs and government assistance.

As Ty got older, he understood his mother's struggle to the point where he took it upon himself to make it better in their household. Knowing he had to be the man of the house, he stepped up, hit the block, and imitated the old hustlers who stood on the corner night and day slinging crack. Before long, he was flipping eight-balls and quarter ounces. He and Tony hit the block day after day determined to get paid.

"You're welcome Ma. Love you." Ty released the embrace he had on his mother, removed the necklace from the box, walked behind her, and placed the beautiful pendant around her neck.

"Happy birthday Mrs. Mae."

"Thank you, baby."

Bianca was at a loss for words as she witnessed the special moment between mother and son. What she felt for Ty before they visited his mother had just gotten deeper.

As Ty fastened the necklace around his mother's neck, he looked over at Bianca and blew her a kiss.

"That is beau—" Bianca's words were cut off by a knock at the door.

Knock! Knock! Knock!

"I'll get it," Ty said, then headed to the door, leaving Mrs. Mae and Bianca to get acquainted.

Knock! Knock! Knock!

"Hold up!" Ty screamed, wondering who was impatiently knocking on his mother's door.

When he reached the door, he snatched it open, ready to

scream at whoever was on the other side banging.

"Damn, nigga, open the door!" Tony barked playfully, standing there with a big shopping bag.

"Quit beatin' like the feds then nigga," Ty snapped back as he gave Tony dap.

Mrs. Mae was like a mother to Tony, and every year on her birthday, he bought her the same gift, a wool sweater with a matching scarf.

Tony headed straight to the kitchen. When he saw Bianca, his heart fluttered. He tried his best not to let his facial expression reveal his true feelings as he looked into the eyes of the woman who he was still crazy in love with.

Bianca had ended their relationship over six months ago because of his excessive partying and wild lifestyle. He heard in the streets that she and Ty had been seeing each other, but he never questioned Ty about it. However, seeing her in the kitchen with Mrs. Mae let him know they were closer than close, especially since Ty wasn't the one to just bring any female to his mother's crib.

"Ma! Happy birthday!" Tony called out, while handing Mrs. Mae the bag and discreetly rolling his eyes at Bianca, who returned his distaste with a frown.

"Thanks, baby!" Mrs. Mae dug inside the bag and pulled out the sweater.

"Nice," Ty commented as he entered the kitchen. He immediately picked up on the vibe between Tony and Bianca. "Ma, we gotta be heading out. Got a few errands to run. I'll call you later. Tony, hit me up later so we can make our presence felt at Club Shampoo tonight," Ty told him as he pulled his keys from his pocket.

"It was nice meeting you." Bianca smiled and shook Mrs. Mae's hand, then exited the kitchen, walking in front of Ty.

"You, too, Bianca. Come see me again."

"Okay, Ma, I gotta get outta here, too. I'll be talking to you."

"Okay, baby, but you get back over here to see me soon. You hear me?"

"I'll do that." Tony gave Mrs. Mae a hug and kiss before following behind Ty and Bianca. "Say, Ty, I need to holla at you," he called out.

After they exited the house, Bianca took the keys from Ty and got in the car while Tony pulled Ty to the side. Ty hoped his boy wasn't about to question him about his relationship with Bianca. He knew the history between Tony and Bianca, and he also knew she had just been a side jawn to Tony, which ultimately resulted in her calling it quits with him. Ty had never spoken about their current situation because he figured it wouldn't be an issue with Tony.

"Man, I need you. Shit's tight for me out here," Tony said, knowing he was already in the red with Ty for over nine thousand dollars.

Sticking his hands in his pockets, he looked at Tony and asked, "What's up fam? What's going on?"

"I had to toss a half a brick last night, and I'm short on the re-up. I need a jumpstart. Need a whole thang to get back on my feet and take care of our tab. I need a brick and a week, straight up," Tony explained.

Ty knew Tony well. Therefore, he knew he had fucked up his money in the mall or the strip club on some trick bitches. This was his third jumpstart, as Tony called it, and Ty had lost on each one. He loved Tony like a brother, but he knew if he kept giving him fronts, he would never get right. Ty told himself this would be his last time fronting him, but he was going to make Tony sweat a little first.

"I got three whole ones, but they already gone. I'll be copping next week, so just lay low 'til then. I got you," Ty told him, then looked at his watch.

"Just let me get one of them fam, because I'm on my dick, for real."

Even though Tony was speaking with emphasis, Ty was un-moved.

"Next week on the work, bro. I'll hit you tonight when I get ready to hit Club Shampoo," Ty said.

He then turned and headed to his car where Bianca sat behind the wheel waiting. She had been watching them through the rearview mirror, and therefore, she saw what Ty hadn't seen, which was the scowl on Tony's face as Ty walked off. It spoke volumes.

"Let's ride," Ty said when he got in.

"Everything okay?" she asked, looking through the mirror at Tony as he jumped in his late-model Chrysler 300. Every time she saw Tony, she was glad she was no longer with him. He looked good with his smooth skin and fresh cut but, he never made her feel special the way Ty did.

"Yeah, everything's good," he replied as they pulled off.

Tony refused to wait around for next week. As he navigated his Chrysler through the South Philly streets, he thought of a plan.

TONYSTORY

CHAPTER 2

TONYSTORY

G STREET CHRONICLES
~A NEW URBAN DYNASTY~

WWW.GSTREETCHRONICLES.COM

A few hours later, Tony ran into Zack, one of his old friends from the neighborhood who was looking for some work. This made Tony switch up his original plans.

"Boy, I been hearing big thangs about you and Ty. I appreciate you fucking wit' me on short notice," Zack told Tony.

They were sitting in Tony's ride with half a block of synthetic dope.

"I'm going to tell Ty to get at you too. Straight up, my nigga, this is that good. You gonna have them country niggas blowing your phone up," Tony told Zack, while handing him the tightly wrapped half-brick of fake dope.

Zack had traveled up from North Carolina, where he had relocated, looking for a half a brick that Ace, his down south buyer, had paid him for in advance. Just his luck, or at least he thought it was luck, Zack bumped into Tony, who was looking for a sweet lick. He never questioned Tony about the package that he had just turned over to him. Since the three of them had grown up together, Zack had a level of trust for him. Besides,

Ty was "The Man" around the city and he knew how close he and Tony were.

"Good looking out bro. I'll be hittin' you when I'm ready to re-up. Shit, I'll hit the road all day, every day at these prices." Zack loved the price tag his old friend had just given him on the play, which was thirteen thousand five hundred dollars.

Tony reached over and dapped him up, rushing him out the car.

"That's what's up, fam. I'll be on deck. Just hit me." Tony watched as Zack exited his car and climbed back into his Chevy Suburban with the small bag containing the imitation product.

Zack, who found that the money down south was easier to touch than it was in Philly, had taken his campaign to North Carolina. He made most of his money being the middleman. Since his current connect was out of town, he decided to go back up north in search of a good deal so he could make some top money off of the deal. He was charging the dealers in the city eighteen thousand dollars for a half a brick and thirty-six thousand dollars for a whole one. His old connect was giving him a half for fifteen thousand five hundred dollars and the whole for thirty-two thousand dollars. So, bumping into Tony had almost doubled his profit.

Zack phoned Ace on his way back down the highway.

"I'll be by the pool hall around eleven o'clock. I'll hit you when I'm almost there so you can be outside, 'cause I'll be on the move," he told Ace, one of Carolina's up and coming hustlers.

"A'ight playa," Ace replied. Being that it was a drought in the streets of Carolina, he was anxiously waiting to get his hands on the dope.

Eight hours later, Zack exited the expressway and made a right on Washington Street where the local pool hall was located. After passing through the third traffic light, he then made a left into the pool hall's parking lot. Ace stood outside by his car smoking a Newport. He took two more hard pulls on the cigarette, stubbed it out with his shoe and walked toward Zack's truck.

"Yo, playa, what we looking like?" Ace asked as he opened the truck door and climbed in the passenger seat.

"The half, what you ordered—all eighteen ounces weighed up," Zack responded, grabbing the bag that contained the package from the back seat.

"Boy, we loving you down here. I'll be getting at ya." Ace smiled, displaying a mouth full of gold teeth as he grabbed the package from Zack, handed him the money, bumped fists with him, and jumped out the truck.

"Just get at me when you ready to re-up."

Ace got in his beat-up, old-school, looked around, and then opened the package. His heart dropped as he looked down at something that resembled cocaine, but he could tell right away it was far from the real shit.

"That fuck nigga!" he barked. He broke the package open and saw that he had been got.

Snatching his glock .40 from under the seat, he jumped out his car. Zack was bringing the truck's engine to life when Ace snatched the door open.

"Nigga, you tried me!" Ace spat.

Not giving Zack a chance to say one word, he raised the gun and pulled the trigger, sending a flurry of hollow-point bullets through his body. Zack's body jerked violently, then fell over in the passenger seat. He died not knowing why Ace had pumped his body full of bullets.

Meanwhile, in Philly, Tony walked through the mall looking for something to wear to Club Shampoo later that night. He never thought twice about serving his old friend the fake package that ultimately cost him his life. Tony didn't care; all he cared about was the come up.

TONY STORY

CHAPTER 3

TONY STORY

G STREET CHRONICLES
~A NEW URBAN DYNASTY~

WWW.GSTREETCHRONICLES.COM

Club Shampoo was packed; all the ballers and hustlers were out. Tony and Ty pulled up to the valet in Ty's black customized Porsche Panamera.

"Damn, boy, it's some bad hoes in this bitch tonight," Tony said, eyeing the females standing in the club's long line wearing short skirts and tights.

"Boy, I see. This shit crazy," Ty replied, as the valet opened his door and held it for him as he climbed out dressed in the latest gear.

Ty stepped out in a black and green Gucci ensemble that he topped off with a platinum diamond necklace that sparkled in sync with the diamond-filled Rolex on his wrist. The ladies in line were in no way discreet with their stares and whispers. They were like hungry wolves stalking prey. Ty noticed the attention they were getting, but played it off like he didn't as he started toward the door.

"These hoes looking for the business tonight," Tony added, also picking up on the ladies gazing at them.

Tony brushed down his Fendi shirt and Dsquared jeans that he had just purchased earlier from the mall with the money he made off Zack. His chain, with its diamond-studded Jesus piece, gave off a dim sparkle and had cost him half the money he had hit Zack for. When Ty picked Tony up and laid his eyes on Tony's new attire, he instantly knew where his money was going.

Ty would stay true to his word this time, but if Tony didn't handle this next brick like a true hustler, he planned to write the loss and him off. He had given Tony work on top of work, but he just kept fucking up the money. So, now he had no choice.

On the flip side, Tony felt like he grinded day in and day out only to turn all of the profits over to Ty, who he felt should be showing him way more love.

"Let's go in this bitch and show them how South Philly does it," Ty told Tony as they walked to the front of the line. "Hugo, what's the deal?" Ty said to the bouncer, who he knew well from past visits. He then reached in his pocket, pulled out a hundred dollar bill and slid it to him.

"Same old shit, money. Y'all enjoy." Hugo waved them in and signaled the girl who was collecting the money at the door to let her know they were VIP and didn't have to pay.

As soon as they entered, the Rick Ross/Meek Mill song "So Sophisticated" pierced their ears. Looking around the packed room, they noticed diamonds reflecting in the lights, bottles raised in the air, and scantily clad women trying to bag a baller. Tony and Ty made their way through the crowded club and headed to VIP.

"Made man!" Cato, a North Philly D-boy called out as Ty walked by.

Ty knew only one person who addressed him by that name.

He turned toward the voice and Cato, his young protégé from the old hood, held his hand up for some dap.

"Boy, what's up! Nigga, how you living!" Ty shouted over the club's sound system as he embraced his old friend.

"You know how I'm living…good," Cato said, giving himself a onceover in a boastful way to make sure Ty saw the flashy jewels he wore.

"Okay, I see you," Ty commented as he stepped back, checking out the young hustler he had put on years ago.

"What up, Tony?" he asked dryly before reaching over and slapping hands with him. Cato would never forget when Tony held him at gunpoint for selling dope on his block.

"What up lil' nigga?" Tony responded with a smirk, then turned his attention back to the crowd.

"Boy, we 'bout to hit this VIP. You drinking?" Ty asked as the club went wild when TI's new song "G Season" came on.

"Man, I'm 'bout to bounce. Gotta catch up with this lil' broad on the south side. What's your digits so we can catch up on some biz, 'cause I know you still making shit happen," Cato said, while pulling out his phone.

After giving Cato his number, Ty made his way through the crowd to the VIP section with Tony by his side. A bunch of groupies were crowded around a cluster of South Philly players. Ty gave the bouncer at the rope a hundred dollar bill, and he unlatched the rope so they could enter.

"Say, beautiful, could you get us two of them?" Ty called out, pointing to an empty bottle of Ace of Spades sitting on a table.

"Okay. Anything else?" The young, well-built waitress made it obvious that she liked what she saw. She looked Ty up and down, checking him out thoroughly.

"Nah, that's it," he answered.

Ty noticed two of the females from the group of women being entertained by the players looking in their direction and whispering.

Tony checked out two half-clothed stallions as they walked by down below. "Yo, Ms. Lady," he called out, motioning for them to come up to VIP.

The two women looked up at him, said something to each other, smiled, and made their way up to the VIP section.

For the next couple of hours, they entertained the women, talked big-money talk with old hustlers and players, and made some connections.

"Boy, I'm out of it," Ty told Tony when they finally decided to call it a night.

"You ain't the only one. Man, I still need that whole thang. You got a nigga or what?" Tony asked as they stood out front waiting for the valet to bring the car around.

Suddenly, there was a loud commotion at the door of the club. They both turned around just in time to see the bouncer throw two dike bitches out onto the street.

Just then, the valet pulled up.

"Nigga, I told you next week. Just chill, my nigga. I got you," Ty slurred, while climbing behind the wheel of the Porsche.

"Boy, you really handling a nigga like a sucker," Tony blurted out, letting the liquor talk.

"Sucker? How in the hell am I handling you like a sucker when you owe me?" Ty snapped back.

"It's all good. Don't even trip it. I'll lay low 'til next week. Say no more," Tony said, then turned up the radio and laid his head back on the seat.

During the rest of the ride not a word was spoken between the two.

TONY STORY

CHAPTER 4

G STREET CHRONICLES
A NEW URBAN DYNASTY

WWW.GSTREETCHRONICLES.COM

The next day, Tony sat in his Northside apartment counting the remaining money from the Zack lick.

"Fuck," he grumbled as he counted out a little less than thirty-five hundred dollars.

After recounting the money a second time, he realized he hadn't counted wrong. He'd spent a considerable amount more at the mall on the clothes and new white gold chain than he thought he did. As he folded the money and wrapped a rubber band around it, his bedroom door flew open.

"Give it up, nigga!" his little brother, LB, shouted as he busted in his room wearing a mask and holding a loaded Colt .45.

Looking up, Tony didn't flinch.

"Nigga, put that shit up and quit playing. I done told yo' young ass!" Tony snapped.

Tony was LB's idol. When you looked at the two of them you couldn't really tell they were brothers, except when you looked in their eyes. Tony was tall and thin while LB was shorter and out of shape. LB tried to mimic everything he saw his big brother do. At the age of seventeen, LB was a straight up menace. He had turned to the streets at an early age and tried his hand at selling dope, but he felt more comfortable being a stick-up kid. His profession had already garnered him two bodies under his belt and numerous aggravated assaults. Tony had always tried to steer his little brother in the opposite direction of the lifestyle which he lived, but he wouldn't take heed. After realizing he was set on living that life, Tony gave up trying and instead sat LB down to teach him the game of the streets.

"Oh, so you think I'm playin', nigga?" LB called out, pushing the gun closer to Tony's face.

"Nigga, didn't I tell you!" Tony barked. Then, moving quickly, he snatched the gun away from LB and turned it on him.

"Damn, homie, you got it!" Holding his hands in the air, LB laughed.

Tony snatched LB's mask off and threw it across the room, then handed him back the gun. Tony had practically raised LB after their mother was sucked in by the streets. Their mother, Ms. Cathy, got hooked on heroin not long after the birth of LB, which was right after their father was sentenced to life for robbery and a double murder.

LB's upbringing was different from Tony's. Even though Tony hadn't been born with a silver spoon in his mouth, he was blessed with more than the average kids in his hood thanks to Ms. Cathy's many years of working with SEPTA. LB, on the other hand, was brought up during the time when Ms. Cathy no longer had a job due to the economic crunch, which forced the city to lay off a lot of their more tenured employees.

Things didn't start to get really bad for them until a slick player from Newark introduced her to heroin. After that, she chased a high all the way to an early grave. One day after school, LB found his mother unresponsive, and ever since her death, Tony had been the sole provider for his little brother. Tony raised LB with the help of the streets, and that's why he couldn't complain when LB embraced the streets the same as he had done.

"Lil' nigga, what you got going on?" Tony asked him, raising up off the bed.

"Shit. Creeping on a come up, nigga. 'Bout to run to the Chinese store for some more blunts. Give a nigga some of that Kush you holding," LB said, already high on Kush and Lean.

"Go grab the blunts and I'll burn one with you," Tony said, picking up his phone to call Ty's cousin Paulie, who had the whole Philly on lock.

"Bet that." LB tucked his gun in his waist while walking out of the room high as a kite.

Paulie answered on the second ring.

"Speak," Paulie said, not recognizing Tony's number.

"Yo, Paulie, this Tony. What it do?" Tony asked, pulling the bag of Kush from the nightstand drawer.

"What up, T? What's up wit' ya?" Paulie knew Tony's call carried a motive.

"Man, you know if I'm hitting you, it's urgent. I went to Ty first, but he all dry. I need a favor, dawg, real talk." Tony grabbed the wad of money from on top of the nightstand.

"What up?" Paulie asked curiously.

"I need you to front me four and a baby 'til Ty get back on next week. My nigga, your money all good," Tony solicited.

"Homie, you know I don't even break down like that, but if something on that level fall my way, I'll hit you," Paulie told him.

Tony didn't respond. He just disconnected the line.

* * * * *

LB cut through the back alley and apartments on his way to the Chinese store. As he passed through, he peeped a couple of hustlers shooting dice out front with money scattered in front of them.

"My dice," the old-school con man called out as he watched the young hustlers pick up his money.

LB smiled as he pulled the homemade stocking mask over his face.

"All y'all lay it down!" LB yelled, aiming the Colt .45 at the group of men.

They had been so focused on their crap game that they didn't see or hear LB approaching.

"Come on now, youngin'," the old school hustler said as he slowly stood. He was mentally calculating the distance between his hand and the .357 Python he had tucked in the small of his back.

All three men were boxed in with nowhere to turn.

"It's all good, money," the short, fat hustler called out as he kicked the stack of bills on the ground over toward LB.

"Now empty ya pockets and take them pieces off!" LB screamed from behind the mask.

Right then, he was floating on some Kush and Lean and really didn't give a fuck.

The third man watched LB's eyes intently, and as soon as his gaze shifted, he took off running, which was a bad decision. The fire shot three inches from the barrel of the Colt, knocking the man clean off his feet. He lay with a big smoking hole in his midsection.

"Shit, man! Here!" the fat man yelled, his voice shaking as he looked over at his brother sprawled out dead in the grass.

Fat man quickly emptied his pockets and stripped off his jewelry while the old-school hustler did the same. The hustler knew the lil' nigga with the gun had no plans on leaving them breathing. He frantically emptied his pockets while at the same time reaching around for his .357. The Lean and Kush caused LB's reaction time to be five seconds too slow. The old-school hustler snatched the gun from his back and let off three shots, barely missing LB.

A shocked LB let loose the Colt that sounded like a cannon going off.

Boom! Boom!

LB stumbled backwards letting off a few wild shots. The fat man spit up blood as he struggled to breathe after a slug hit him in the chest. Still on his feet, the old-school hustler continued to bust pointless shots at LB as he fled.

TONY STORY

CHAPTER 5

G STREET CHRONICLES
~A NEW URBAN DYNASTY~

WWW.GSTREETCHRONICLES.COM

The next day, Ty stood in the kitchen of his townhouse trying to adjust the mechanical scale. He pulled two bricks from the garage and prepared to break them down for the four half-brick sales and three, four-and-a-half orders. With the product moving fast, Ty knew before long he would be contacting his connect for his biggest order ever. He only had two whole kilos left to sell and one for Tony on the front. He didn't even tally up the take on that one because when dealing with Tony nothing was ever guaranteed. As he finished adjusting the scale, his cell phone vibrated on the table.

"Yeah?" he answered, cuffing the phone between his face and shoulder as he cut the thick tape containing the block of cocaine.

"You still ain't fucking wit' ya fam, my nigga?" Tony asked jokingly, but at the same time, he was serious while pacing back and forth in his apartment hoping Ty would reconsider.

"Damn, bro, I keep telling you the same thang…next week. I'm sitting here right now putting together the last of the package.

Niggas already had orders in, fam," Ty said sternly.

Hearing the panic in Tony's voice, Ty smiled to himself knowing he had a kilo sitting to the side in the garage for Tony.

"Ty, I got 'bout three stacks to my name, and my rent and other bills 'bout to kill that. Boy, I need that thang bad or just give me a half. Shit, it don't matter right now," Tony pressed, trying his best not to sound like he was begging. He knew when he paid his bills, he would be practically broke.

"Next week," Ty repeated before ending the call.

Tony tossed his phone on the bed, walked over to the closet, and grabbed his jacket. On his way out the door, he snatched up his keys and his Beretta .9mm from off the counter.

As he cruised down Broad Street, he grabbed the half-smoked blunt from the ashtray and lit it. By the time he made the right on Carpenter Street, the blunt had burned to a roach, and he was floating on cloud nine from the potent Kush. When he got to Ty's place, he pulled up between his BMW and Porsche and killed the engine on his 300. Pushing the car door open, he stepped out with an obvious bulge under his jacket. His mind raced and heart pumped hard as he approached the door.

Ding! Ding!

Ty jumped when his doorbell chimed. He looked around the kitchen for a quick place to tuck the dope and scale. After hurriedly stashing the dope and scale under the kitchen cabinet, he rushed to the door wondering who the hell could be out front. He had talked to Bianca and she was at home. Paulie wouldn't have just dropped by without calling first, and no one else knew where he laid his head. As he peeped out the blinds, he saw Tony, the one person he forgot about.

Ty snatched open the door and yelled, "Nigga, didn't I just

hang up the phone with you!" By this point, he decided to go ahead and give Tony the kilo, knowing by his persistence that he must have really been in a serious bind.

Ty moved to the side and let Tony in, then locked the door behind them.

"Shit tight for real," Tony said in a sinister tone as they made their way to the kitchen.

"Man, you need to handle the next move like a real hustler. Flip that shit and double up, 'cause man, you supposed to be straight. Nigga, I don't want to feed you. I want you to eat with me," Ty said as he retrieved the drugs and scale from under the counter and placed them back on the table.

"Yeah, I know," Tony replied, eyeing the big blocks of raw cocaine.

Ty had to make him sweat one more time before sending him to the garage to get the kilo he had set to the side for him.

"This is the last of the last, fam. You'll be straight next week," Ty said, while lowering his head to keep Tony from seeing the smile he was trying hard to hold back.

He waited for Tony's rebuttal, but it never came. An eerie silence hovering over the room made Ty look up at his friend. His heart dropped when he found himself looking down the barrel of Tony's .9mm.

"Ay, bro, what the fuck?" Ty asked, a look of shock and surprise appearing on his face.

He didn't totally panic because he knew his best friend, his brother from another mother, wouldn't shoot him.

"My nigga, it's time for me to eat, and I ain't talkin' 'bout them crumbs you been bird feeding a nigga wit'," Tony barked, holding the gun sideways in a tight grip.

"Crumbs? You can't be serious, my nigga. T, you tripping. Put that shit down and grab that brick out the garage," Ty said shakily, with beads of sweat forming on his brow as he pushed his chair back from the table and stood erect.

"Nigga, you ain't really fucking wit' me," Tony said calmly in a dark tone.

"Nigga, like I said, you tripping!" Ty spat, now becoming angry because Tony hadn't lowered his gun.

Ty couldn't believe it had come to this, but he knew he couldn't just stand there. He needed to get to his .40 Heckler & Koch on the counter and show Tony who he was dealing with.

"Nah, you tripping!" Tony yelled as he tightened his grip and pulled the trigger.

Pop! Pop! Pop! Pop!

All the hate, envy, and jealousy seeped out of Tony as he flicked the trigger on the gun until all sixteen shots pierced Ty's body. Ty jerked from side to side as each bullet found a resting spot. He swatted at the hollow points as if he could block them. Ty couldn't believe his childhood friend was pumping shots into him. After seconds of fighting to live, Ty tumbled over the chair and fell to the floor.

Tony stepped around the table and surveyed the damage he'd done to his friend. After seeing that Ty was no longer breathing, he reached down, snatched the Rolex off his wrist, took the money out his pockets, then quickly bagged up the drugs from the table and did a quick search of the house. He was happy to have found more drugs and cash. This was the type of lick he needed.

On his way out the house, he smiled as he suddenly remembered Ty's other stash, which was kept at Ms. Mae's spot.

TONY STORY

CHAPTER 6

G STREET CHRONICLES
~A NEW URBAN DYNASTY~

WWW.GSTREETCHRONICLES.COM

"**D**amn, somebody really hated this guy. This is definitely not your average kitchen. Look over there at that equipment. From the looks of that scale, this guy was dealing in some heavy stuff," Detective Johansen stated, as the other CSI officials examined the crime scene.

"Yeah, whoever did this must have hated his guts," the assisting detective on the scene added, while noting the number of times Ty had been shot.

"No signs of drugs, but from the look of the paraphernalia on the table, more than likely some was present. Write it up as a drug-related murder and armed robbery. I need you to make sure you detail the report with everything you find here. I'm going to talk to the lady who called this in," Johansen said, then exited the kitchen. He made his way outside where Bianca was crying hysterically after finding Ty lying in a pool of his own blood.

*****

Bianca had called Ty over ten times. She had been waiting outside of Posh Hair Palace for him to pick her up. It wasn't like Ty not to answer his phone or be late, so she kept calling his cell phone. After many failed attempts to reach him, she gave up and called a cab. Upon arriving at his townhouse, she felt disrespected when she noticed both of his cars parked out front. Fuming, she paid the fare, climbed out the cab, and slammed the door.

"This is some bullshit," Bianca said as she rushed up to the door, ready to cuss Ty's ass out.

She banged on the door for all of five minutes, but he never answered. After standing out front for another five minutes, she reached out and tried the doorknob. To her surprise, it was unlocked. She opened the door, and instantly, a funny smell made her squinch her nose. Not familiar with the smell of death, she entered the house calling out Ty's name. She went upstairs first, but saw that he wasn't in his room. After checking upstairs and not finding him, she went back downstairs and made her way to the kitchen. She had a funny feeling something was wrong.

As she crossed the room, she couldn't believe what she saw. Her heart dropped, and she screamed at the top of her lungs. Ty lay stiff and lifeless in a pool of blood. Bianca wasn't sure what to do. She wanted to lift him up in hopes that somehow he'd start breathing again, but she couldn't. There was so much blood and the stench was so horrible that she started throwing up. Then she turned and rushed out of the house screaming while dialing 911 on her cell phone. The neighbors and other tenants trickled out of their homes to see what was going on.

Before long, Philadelphia Police were on the scene sectioning off the townhouse with yellow "Crime Scene" tape and getting prepared to start their murder investigation.

*****

"Hi, ma'am. Sorry for your loss. I'm Detective Johansen. What's your name?"

Johansen took a position beside her next to Ty's BMW.

Using the back of her hand, she wiped her tears before speaking.

"B...Bianca Rawls," she stuttered and sniffed, while wiping at her tears again.

"Well, Bianca, I'm going to find out who's responsible for this. How are you related to the man inside?" he asked as he leaned against Ty's BMW.

"Ty's my...my boyfriend," she said, struggling to get the words out through her heavy breathing.

"Okay, so his name is Ty? Do you know if he had any enemies or was involved in anything illegal?" He pulled his pen and pad from his pocket, ready to jot down any information that could possibly help solve the case.

"No, he was a good person. He ain't have no enemies, and he wasn't doing nothing illegal," Bianca lied, burying her face in her hands.

She knew his drug dealing was likely the reason he was dead.

"Well, it looks as if someone came to rob him for whatever he was dealing in, and during the robbery, they killed him. What really has me stumped, though, is the overkill involved. Whoever killed this man had a lot of malice in their heart towards him,"

Johansen said as he scribbled something illegible on the notepad.

"God, I don't know." Bianca broke down and started to shake as she cried uncontrollably.

Johansen rose up from off of the car.

"I'm sorry, ma'am. We'll do everything we can to get to the bottom of this. Do you have information of his next of kin?" he asked, readying his pen to write.

Before Bianca could answer, a black Cadillac ESV whipped in the lot two cars over from the BMW. Mrs. Mae slung the door open and slowly climbed out as Paulie hurried out behind her. Just as they were nearing the scene, they looked up and saw the coroners wheeling Ty's body out on a gurney, completely concealed in a black body bag.

"Nooo! My baby!" Mrs. Mae screamed, then dropped to her knees as Bianca and Paulie rushed to her side.

Detective Johansen followed behind Bianca, and as soon as he reached them, he locked eyes with Paulie, who returned the gaze. Their look was that of two people who were somehow familiar with one another even though they were on opposite sides of the track.

* * * * *

The days leading up to Ty's funeral were extremely hard and stressful for Mrs. Mae. She had continuous support from her family, friends, church family, neighbors, and of course, Paulie, who made sure his cousin was laid to rest the way he should be.

The church was filled with family, friends, hustlers, groupies, and everyone else who knew Ty. Tony sat on the front pew holding Mrs. Mae, with Bianca by her side.

"Ma, it's going to be alright. I promise you, I'm going to get whoever did this to Ty," Tony told her firmly as she wiped her tears in agreement, dismissing her religion.

Paulie had dropped by the church earlier in the day so he could have some time to speak his final words to his cousin Ty alone. He left before all the other people arrived to pay their last respects to a man well liked and admired in the streets.

"This ain't right!" Mrs. Mae screamed as they pulled the cloth over Ty's face and closed the casket.

Tony and the other pallbearers positioned themselves on both sides of the casket to carry it to the hearse. Tony almost dropped the .9mm tucked in his waist...the same one he used to end Ty's existence.

Tony had one of his boys drive his car to the cemetery while he climbed into the limo with Mrs. Mae and Bianca. They rode in silence as they followed the hearse. There was a long line of cars in the procession to Lincoln Cemetery, which would be Ty's final resting place. Mrs. Mae was a wreck; her heart was heavy and her breathing became shallow.

Once inside the cemetery's gates, the funeral directors located Ty's plot and the procession came to a halt. Mrs. Mae remained in the car while Tony and the pallbearers resumed their positions and carried the casket over to the six-feet-deep hole that would envelope Ty soon after the ceremony.

Tony returned to the limo and escorted Mrs. Mae to the gravesite, with Bianca following behind. Mrs. Mae insisted Bianca stay close to her. The last memory she had of her son was when he and Bianca had visited her and gave her a beautiful pendant, the same pendant she was proudly wearing on the worst day of her life...the day she had to bury her son.

Mrs. Mae was in a daze through most of the service. She still couldn't believe this was happening. She waited for someone to wake her from what she wished was a nightmare, but it didn't happen.

The preacher brought her out of her trance when he bellowed while throwing speckles of dirt on the light blue metallic casket. "Ashes to ashes, dust to dust."

"Noooooo!" Mrs. Mae screamed, then crumbled to the ground holding her chest.

"Call 911!" Bianca screamed to the onlookers who had accompanied them to the gravesite.

Ten minutes later, Mrs. Mae was being rushed to the hospital in the back of an ambulance. She never had the chance to pay her last respects to her loving son.

Tony insisted Bianca go back in the limo. He got his keys from his boy and followed close behind the ambulance, unmoved by all that had happened. He was just ready to get the day over with because he had dope to flip.

TONY STORY

CHAPTER 7

G STREET CHRONICLES
~A NEW URBAN DYNASTY~

WWW.GSTREETCHRONICLES.COM

"Yo, anybody 'round your way been all of a sudden dumping white for the low?" Paulie asked Lance, one of his buyers from North Philly.

"Naw, not that I heard of. Why? What's up?" he asked curiously.

"Somebody hit my cousin up, and I know they got off with a nice piece of work," Paulie said, reflecting back on his conversation with Detective Johansen that night outside of Ty's house when he informed him of what was and wasn't found at the murder scene.

"Word? Damn, they did that shit over…" Lance started.

"Yeah, my nigga, and best believe I'm going to find out who was behind it," Paulie said with a hint of anger in his tone.

"If I hear anything, I'll hit you up. I got my ear to the street," Lance told him, knowing Paulie was one to stand on his word and wouldn't let up until he found out who was responsible.

"Good looking out," Paulie said as he ended the call. Next, he dialed Tony's number.

Tony had just left the hospital with Mrs. Mae and was on his way to take her home after she had been treated for what they thought may have been a mild heart attack, but actually turned out to be an anxiety attack. Mrs. Mae sat silently in the passenger seat holding her prescribed pills as they made their way through the dark Philly streets.

As Tony made a left onto her block, his cell phone rang.

"Yeah," Tony answered, while pulling into the driveway of Mrs. Mae's house.

"What up, Tony? Did you hear anything at the funeral about Ty's murder?" Paulie asked, knowing a lot of hustlers from around the way had been in attendance.

"Naw, fam, everybody still guessing. After I drop Ma Mae off, I'm going through the old hood to see what I can dig up. They thought Ma had a mild heart attack today at the funeral, but it was some kind of anxiety attack or something like that. We just now getting back to her house, but she alright now," Tony explained as he killed the engine.

"Anxiety attack? She good?" Paulie asked in a concerned tone.

"She good, man. They say she has to rest though, because it could've been worse if we hadn't gotten her to the hospital so fast. I'm dropping her off now," he said while getting out and rushing around to help her out the car.

"Well, keep me posted, and tell Auntie I'll be through tomorrow to check on her," Paulie told Tony before ending the call with his mind still racing.

Tony walked Mrs. Mae up to the door and used her key to open it.

"You good, Ma?" he asked when they stepped in the dark, cold house.

"Yeah, I'm okay. Just a little woozy," Mrs. Mae said. She spoke as if out of breath as she walked slowly through the house.

Tony knew Ty had another stash somewhere in the house. He paused for a minute to think back on the last time Ty mentioned putting money up in the house...

"Boy, what you got going on stashing all your lil' secrets in my closet," Mrs. Mae told Ty as he carried the fifteen thousand dollars he had just picked up earlier from Loco, his Mexican buyer.

That day, Tony had been sitting on the couch scrolling through his contact list, looking for a potential sale for the front he had just got.

Tony helped Mrs. Mae up the stairs and into her bedroom. Knowing the stash was in the closet, he looked around for an excuse to go in it.

"Lay down, Ma. I'll get you something comfortable to put on," Tony told her, as he passed her dresser and went straight to the closet.

"I'm fine right now, baby. I'm just going to lay down for a minute or two." She kicked off her flats, laid her prescription on her nightstand, and climbed into the bed.

Adamant about finding the stash, Tony disregarded her refusal and stepped into the closet anyway. He moved around a few pieces of clothing and found three Timberland shoeboxes stacked in the corner behind a shopping bag. He bent down, opened the top box, and was greeted with stacks of rubber-banded bills. He then proceeded to look in the other two boxes, and in the midst of his rummaging, he heard Mrs. Mae call out from the bed.

"Tony, what you doing in there?" she asked, tilting her head up to look toward the closet.

Soon after she called out, she sat all the way up in the bed and saw Tony exiting the closet with the boxes that contained the money Ty had been stashing.

"It's all good, Ma. Just grabbing a lil' something," Tony said.

"Tony, put that back. That's not yours! What are you doing?" Mrs. Mae asked, trying to catch her breath.

"Rest, Ma. It's more to this than you know," he told her, then started out the room with the boxes of money.

"Tony, put those boxes back!" Mrs. Mae yelled as she kicked one leg off the bed and proceeded to get up.

"I'll call you later, Ma," he called out and kept walking.

She struggled to get off of the bed, and before she could gain her footing, she started gasping for air and holding her chest. When Tony heard her breathing heavily, he turned around to see what was going on. Seconds later, Mrs. Mae fell to the floor holding her chest. Her breathing was quick and hard, and her body was shaking. Clutching at her chest, Mrs. Mae pleaded with her eyes for Tony to help her.

Tony looked over at the phone on the nightstand and contemplated calling 911, but quickly dismissed the thought. Instead, he rushed out the house and back to his car.

She knew when he rushed out the bedroom and closed the door behind him that it was over. As she looked up at Ty's picture that sat on her dresser, she took her last breath.

TONYSTORY

CHAPTER 8

TWO WEEKS LATER

G STREET CHRONICLES
~A NEW URBAN DYNASTY~

WWW.GSTREETCHRONICLES.COM

"**D**addy, we appreciate you," Kee and Trina told Tony as they walked with him, one on each arm, through the King of Prussia Mall.

Tony was out putting on and enjoying his newfound wealth. He had just spent over ten thousand dollars in Neiman's and was now on the way to the jewelry store to buy himself a new piece.

Two weeks had passed since Ty's death, and Tony was quickly becoming the man in the streets. After flipping the take from Ty, he secured a down south connect who was giving it to him so sweet that other major niggas had to lower their prices just to compete. It didn't take Tony long to build his clientele around the city. The streets knew Ty had been the man, so they figured Tony had inherited his position. Therefore, they started hitting him up, and after getting blow for the low, they became loyal customers. Tony was now serving all of Ty's buyers and even some of the hustlers who were just looking down on him a month ago.

"No need for the thanks beautiful ladies. Y'all deserve this," Tony told them, as Kee tightened her grip on his arm and looked up into his eyes with her hazel contacts.

"I really appreciate you, baby," she said in a seductive tone, while gently digging her long nails into his arms.

Not the one to take the back seat, Trina rubbed her freshly manicured hand across the back of his head and down his neck.

"You really are appreciated, handsome," she added.

Tony smiled from ear to ear. He got comfortable in his new role as they made their way through the mall. Just as they reached the jewelry store, he heard his name being called.

"Yo, Tony!" Paulie called out, rushing up on them.

Tony instinctively positioned his hand to pull the Ruger he had tucked in his waist underneath his shirt.

"What it do, Paulie?" Tony said with a hint of uneasiness in his tone.

Paulie's eyes shot down to the sparkling Rolex glistening on Tony's wrist, the same kind his cousin Ty had owned. He then checked out the new Louis Vuitton gear that Tony sported from head to toe. What really got his attention were the two known gold-digging tricks from North Philly, Kee and Trina, who were holding full Neiman bags. Paulie knew Kee and Trina only fucked with major hustlers, so seeing this little threesome definitely caught him by surprise. Tony had just hit him for a front a couple weeks ago, so Paulie knew something wasn't adding up. But, he kept his composure as he reached out and dapped Tony up, taking him in a half embrace.

"Still trying to make shit jump," Paulie said as he checked Tony out again, contemplating the best revenge since it was obvious Tony had something to do with Ty's murder.

Paulie knew Ty had been holding major work and cash. After checking the scene, no drugs or money were found, which meant it was taken. Now here was Tony splurging like he had hit the lottery after only a few weeks ago begging for some work to get on his feet.

"All day, every day. I'm still on the lookout for the muthafucka responsible for Ty's murder. We both know the streets gonna start talkin' sooner or later," Tony said flatly.

"Yeah, true enough. You know how shit go. What up, Kee… Trina?" Paulie knew the two expensively dressed, well-endowed women didn't come cheap and that Tony was tricking all his cousin's hard-earned street profits on them.

"Hey, Paulie," Kee responded with obvious interest in her tone, still adamant about trying to get into the man's pockets who the hustlers in the city worshiped.

"What up, Paulie," Trina spoke, giving him a seductive stare while running her tongue across her lips.

Paulie had that rough, rugged look that the ladies loved. He was tall and nicely built with beautiful, black wavy hair. He knew he could have either of the women but wasn't interested. He smirked at the women's advances while again thinking about the call weeks ago from Tony asking for a front. Now here he was with deep pockets, splurging and walking through the mall with two of the biggest gold-diggers in the city. Paulie made up his mind right then that Tony had to die.

"Sorry 'bout Mrs. Mae," Tony said, causing Paulie to frown.

Paulie knew Ty's murder was the reason his aunt was now in her final resting place as well.

"Yeah, shit is fucked up. I'll get at you, bro. Ladies, y'all take it easy," Paulie said, while slapping five with Tony and beginning to devise a plan to take him out the game.

Picking up a funny vibe from Paulie as he turned and walked

away, Tony patted the burner concealed under his shirt and then shrugged his shoulders as Kee and Trina held him like he was a paycheck.

TONY STORY

CHAPTER 9

A COUPLE MONTHS LATER

G STREET CHRONICLES
~ A NEW URBAN DYNASTY ~

WWW.GSTREETCHRONICLES.COM

"**N**igga, you been dodging my calls. So, now that we are face to face, you got two choices. Get my money now or eat a bullet," Tony told Cuzzo, while his right-hand man, Brick, held the gun to his face.

"Tony, man, I ain't been dodging you. Just give me a couple more days. You know they just raided my spot a couple days ago. I swear I got you, man," Cuzzo stammered as beads of sweat formed on his large forehead.

Tony walked over and grabbed the pool stick that laid on the brand new tournament-style pool table.

"Yeah, I heard about the raid, but I also know all these new tables and other stuff you just got in here had to cost you a grip…my grip. Really, if you look at it, all this shit in here is my shit. This is my pool room," Tony blurted out as he rounded the table with the custom ivory pool stick, while looking around at all of Cuzzo's newly purchased, expensive furnishings.

Cuzzo hoped his manager would show up soon and interrupt Tony's torment. He knew it had to be close to twelve o'clock, which was the time he was scheduled to be in. Cuzzo prayed he was on time.

"Tony, man, I had already ordered this stuff. I swear, man. I can show you the receipts," Cuzzo said, looking up at Tony from his knees while Brick stood over him unmoved with the .40 Cal in his face.

Tony looked at his watch and then over at Brick.

"A'ight, my nigga, I'm giving you one day to get my money," Tony snapped.

Anticipating Tony's next move, Brick took one step back so the swinging pool stick wouldn't hit him.

"Ahhh, fuck!" Cuzzo screamed out in pain.

The pool stick caught Cuzzo in the back of the head and broke, sending his head forward with his overweight body following behind. He held the back of his head as he curled up in a fetal position on the floor. Tony and Brick moved closer to his fallen body and stood over him.

"One day, nigga. Tomorrow my people here will be back to see you with no understanding," Tony yelled and then tossed the other part of the pool stick at Cuzzo, who was still laid out on the floor.

"Okay, Tony." Cuzzo looked at the two men with pleading eyes as he started to choke.

"Bitch!" Tony spat.

Brick turned to exit the pool hall. He would be leaving soon to head to South Philly to secure the next shipment arriving at two o'clock.

Over the past two months, Tony had become the go-to man in the city. He and his right-hand man Brick, from his old hood, had been setting the city on fire. Tony had it all…the connect, the money, the women, and all the work. Life was good right now for Tony.

* * * * *

Tony and Brick stepped out of the pool hall and headed toward the car. Just as Tony started the engine, a grey Crown Victoria whipped into the lot, blocking their car from exiting.

"Wha...what the hell! Tuck that burner!" Tony quickly said, as Detective Johansen threw the car door open and climbed out.

"How y'all doing today?" Detective Johansen asked, leaning in the driver side window and tapping his finger on the roof of the BMW.

Tony turned off the car before responding. "We good. Just got finished shooting a lil' pool. Is there a problem, Detective?" Tony asked, looking at the detective's badge hanging from the chain around his neck.

"Y'all know Ty? Oh, that's a silly question. Shit, Tony, you know Ty well. Y'all grew up together like brothers. You, Brick, on the other hand, may not have known Ty well since you are a lot younger," the detective said, then paused for effect.

If it were possible, Tony and Brick's faces would've dropped in their laps upon hearing the detective call them by name.

"How..." Tony began, but was cut off when the detective started speaking again.

"Yeah, I'm familiar with the heavyweights out here in these streets. Shit, I *am* a detective. It's my job to know this." Johansen laughed. "I just want to know, Tony, why did you feel you had to kill Ty? Both of us know you did it, but only you know why," Johansen stated, carefully reading Tony's movements and expression.

"What the fuck you saying? That was my fam! You don't know what the hell you..."

Tony stopped midsentence as the detective walked away from the car and climbed back in the Crown Vic.

"Why he kicking that bullshit?" Brick asked, thinking back on Ty who was like a big brother to him.

"That pig don't know what the hell he talking about!" Tony spat as he brought the BMW's engine to life and pulled out the lot.

*****

The ballroom at the Hyatt was packed as the patrons rooted on Nick Foles, who marched the Eagles down the field with under a minute to go after taking Michael Vick's position as quarterback. Big Al, one of Philly's most recognized white-collar hustlers, was having a party, and his guest list boasted only the rich and famous. Sports stars, music stars, and big-time major hustlers filled the room. Al always threw a couple parties a year, and this night was his all-green affair, showing his love for his favorite pastime and football team—the Philadelphia Eagles.

"Damn, that nigga over there got to be rocking a cool million," Kee said, eyeing a slim light-skinned brother standing off in a far corner talking on his cell phone.

"I don't know, girl, but you got to watch them kind. All that shines ain't always a diamond, feel me?" Trina said, looking over at the slim brother who had diamonds draped around his neck and wrists.

"I'm banking on this one." Kee picked up the champagne she'd been sipping on, stood up from the table where they were sitting, and with her glass in her hand, she walked over to the brother.

Kee made sure to put just the right amount of sway in her hips as she strutted over to the man, who was instantly taken in by her wide hips, bowlegs, and thick thighs. Kee was adamant in her conquest as she pushed up on the brother. Standing directly in front of him, she took a seductive sip from her glass of champagne.

"Umm...dang, let me get back at you. When the season starts, you know I got front row seats for you," the brother told the person on the other end of the phone, giving Kee the impression that he was some kind of pro athlete.

Kee sized him up and figured with his big feet, long arms, and slim body, he must be a basketball player.

"Am I interrupting something?" Kee asked, looking up at the man with puppy dog eyes.

"Naw, beautiful, I was just ending my call. I'm Ben, and you are?" He tucked his cell phone in his pocket, never taking his eyes off Kee and barely blinking.

"Ready to go so we can get to know each other," Kee replied with a slick smile.

"The game ain't over yet," Ben said, pointing in the direction of the big screen TV and licking his lips.

"It's over with as far as I'm concerned, especially since I've found something more interesting," Kee replied, then ran her tongue seductively around the rim of her glass.

"I'm feeling that. How 'bout we go up to my room, have a couple drinks, and like you said, get to know each other," he suggested.

"Give me a minute," Kee said, feeling like she had hit the jackpot.

She turned and calmly walked back over to Trina, who was entertaining an expensively-dressed African man at their table.

"Trina, can I speak with you for a minute?" Kee asked, slightly tugging at Trina's arm.

Trina excused herself and the two stepped away from the table.

"What up, Kee? What's light skin talking 'bout?" Trina asked, taking a glance over at Ben, who had his eyes fixated on the two.

"I got me one. This nigga plays for some pro team. We 'bout to go up to his room and have some drinks," Kee told her as she glanced over at the African gentleman.

"Oh shit, that's the move, bitch. But, don't put no hole in that rubber 'til you find out how much he's banking. You know it's time for us to retire, and the hole in the rubber and a good nut is the quickest way to get there!" Trina joked, but was actually dead serious about how they played the game.

"Girl, you know I know!" Kee laughed. "Who's Abdul over there?" she joked, shooting another look at the African man waiting patiently at the table for Trina.

"Oh, him? That's my next Birkin bag and maybe a new car since he owns a couple of car lots."

Kee and Trina shared a laugh before Trina returned to the table, while Kee sashayed back over to Ben.

Thirty minutes later, Kee was on her third shot of Tequila and on her knees.

"Shit!" Ben called out, leaning back on his elbows on the bed, with Kee in front of him giving him slow head, slurping him up.

"Mmmm," Kee moaned, knowing if she sucked him off right he would be hooked.

"Damn…take this off," Ben said while reaching at the

spandex Kee wore.

"Uh-uh," she moaned, refusing his request as she continued to suck him and play with his balls.

"Oh fuck!" Ben gave up and lay all the way back on the bed.

Kee went in hard like a vacuum on fluffy carpet.

Coming up off his shaft, Kee said, "Let me taste it," then quickly resumed her position.

Ben's toes started to curl as his juices rushed to his tip. Kee didn't let up, knowing she had him where she wanted him as he grunted and groaned. She knew this was her intro into a possible role as a basketball wife.

"Uhhhhh!" Ben moaned, releasing inside of her mouth.

Kee took him all in one gulp and then swallowed hard. When she came up, there wasn't a drop to be found. When it came to giving head, she knew her skills could drive a nigga crazy, and after that performance, she knew it was a done deal.

"You good?" she asked, as she rose up and climbed on the bed next to him.

"Shit, ma, you a beast," Ben said, still stuck in the same position.

"That was only for you," Kee replied, reaching over to rub his stomach.

He smiled at her and then sat up. "Damn, I got to be getting back to work," he told her, as he rose up off the bed and started fixing his pants.

"Get back to work? Where you work?" Kee didn't bother to hide her confusion. She knew basketball season didn't start for some months.

"I work for Jay King. You know The King...point man... 76ers. You don't recognize the chain?" Ben held up the chain with the diamond 76ers logo on it.

Kee almost threw up.

"You...you're his assistant? You don't play?" Kee yelled with an attitude.

"Naw. I just carry my people's bags and make sure he's straight," Ben told her, picking up on her changed mood. "You good?"

"Yeah...um, I got to go." Kee picked up her purse and stormed out of the room.

Ben didn't try to stop her or pursue her. He just laughed as she slammed the hotel room door behind her. Then he walked to the front to make sure she was gone before he returned his missed call.

The person on the other end picked up and started talking before Ben could say a word. After listening for a minute, he responded, "Yeah, that sounds good...Nah, I wasn't busy...I can't complain. Shit, I'm just glad to be on the team. One point five million is a start," Ben told his agent, who got him signed to the Philadelphia 76ers after tearing his ACL his first year in the league.

Ben could spot groupies and gold diggers from a mile away, so he knew what was up as soon as Kee walked over to him. He loved the look on their faces when he suddenly became the assistant. Laughing, he finished fixing his clothes and then headed back down to watch the rest of the game.

TONY STORY

CHAPTER 10

TONY STORY

G STREET CHRONICLES
~A NEW URBAN DYNASTY~

WWW.GSTREETCHRONICLES.COM

Paulie cruised through 24th and Somerset looking for Zulu and his sidekick, Peanut. He rode with ten thousand dollars in a bag on the passenger seat, prepared to pay for Tony's demise. After hearing the rumors and gossip about Tony being the go-to man in the city, he picked up his phone and called Tony's number, which he had been trying to reach him on for two months. Still, he got the same result...voicemail.

He circled the block for the third time, and after he had no luck locating Zulu or Peanut, he changed his mind regarding his initial plan on paying to have Tony killed. He went back and forth until he decided he wanted Tony's death on his own hands. He wanted to look into his eyes and watch as he slowly died. To Paulie, that would only be right; he needed to be hands-on for closure.

He stopped at the intersection of 23rd and Lehigh, then made a left and headed back home. On the way there, he got a call from Rico, one of his workers.

"What up, Rico?" Tony asked, not expecting to hear from

Rico until the following week when it was time to pick up and drop off.

"Yo, big homie, that nigga Tony making shit hard to move out here with them prices he giving these niggas. I just had a play for two whole ones, but after quoting the nigga the price, he cut the call short, talking 'bout Ty's homeboy from the Northside with the killer prices. Bruh, this nigga Tony got us stockpiling this shit," Rico said, obviously irritated as hell while looking at the five untouched bricks that Paulie had fronted him last week.

Paulie's blood pressure rose while listening to Rico's words. He wasn't one hundred percent sure that Tony was responsible, but it was a ninety-nine percent chance that he was. Paulie was furious that Tony was living off of his cousin's grind. The streets of Philly were screaming Tony's name hard; he had become a street celebrity in no time. Paulie saw that Tony was not only controlling the dope, but he was also controlling the gangsters and killers. He had become a savior to the city. He showed just enough love to make everyone worship his deeds; he had become a real street politician.

"Yeah, man, I realized that when my connect mentioned it. Shit, he even complaining 'cause shit ain't moving like it was. Now everybody talking about our prices too high, but just a month ago, they were loving the tag we were giving them. My nigga, don't even trip about it. Just jump what you can. Shit going to be back in check in a minute," Paulie assured Rico, while thinking about his plan to make Tony extinct.

"A'ight, I'll get at you if shit changes," Rico told him, attempting to think of the best way to get off the work without dropping the prices to the point where he wouldn't see a profit.

"Yeah, do that." Paulie ended the call, trying his best to hide his overpowering frustration.

* * * * *

"What have you come up with?" Detective Johansen asked his subordinate, Detective Frost, as they sat in their office looking over all the evidence from Ty's murder scene.

"Nothing really stands out at the moment. The evidence shows that the guy was into illegal narcotics. The scale, bags, and residue all over the table were proof of that. It looks as if he was preparing his drugs for distribution and an unexpected visitor popped up or someone was there with him. Whichever way it went, there weren't any signs of forced entry, and the assailant shot and killed the guy for the drugs," Frost explained as the office clerk laid a folder on his desk.

"Yeah, killed him and then robbed him afterwards while he lay in a pool of blood on his own kitchen floor," Johansen added.

"The house had all the signs of being ransacked. Drawers and closets were open, and mattresses flipped. Someone really searched the premises like they were looking for something else. I thought maybe we'd hear something by now from one of our snitches in the area, but ain't nobody talking," Frost said as Johansen thought back on the conversation he had with Tony and Brick, which he hadn't shared with Frost or anyone else for that matter.

"Well, just keep me updated. I got a few leads I'm going to look into myself," Johansen told him, then turned back to his computer and accessed the offender database to look a little deeper into Tony's background.

He was specifically focused on a possible address. After ten minutes of searching the database, he came up empty handed. He saw that Tony had played it cool most of his life, only being convicted of a petty misdemeanor and a couple traffic violations.

"Hey, I think I got something," Frost called out.

He looked at the folder that had just been dropped on his desk, then compared its contents to the information he had up on the computer screen.

"What is it?" Johansen asked, getting up from his desk and walking over to Frost to see what he had discovered.

"Prints! Possible prints of the killer!" Frost said excitedly.

Johansen looked over his shoulder and squinted at the information on the computer screen. The prints belonged to the man on the screen, the same man Johansen had just had on his screen... Tony.

Johansen thought fast.

"Oh yeah, I'm familiar with the guy. He's the man's close friend. I questioned him last week. Frost, where you been? You didn't read my reports?" Johansen lied, playing down Tony's involvement.

"Damn, thought we had something here. Well, back to the drawing board." Frost shrugged as he closed the folder and cleared his screen.

Johansen turned and walked away, planning his next move, which would be much easier if he had an address for Tony.

TONY STORY

CHAPTER 11

G STREET CHRONICLES
~A NEW URBAN DYNASTY~

WWW.GSTREETCHRONICLES.COM

A week later, Paulie pulled up into the Club Onyx parking lot and looked for a parking space amongst the sea of luxury, customized automobiles. His quick assessment of the lot let him know all the heavy hitters were in the house that night. After parking between a matte black Aston Martin with gold rims and a Benz S550, he checked his rearview mirror and exited his Bentley GT. Paulie gave himself a once over and adjusted his pieces so every diamond would get its time to shine under the club's lights. He pressed the button to activate his alarm and stepped from between the cars, walking toward the line of club goers that stretched along the club's outer wall.

"Thick in this bitch tonight," Paulie mumbled to himself as he walked up to the front of the line and motioned for the bouncer, who stood next to the young female collecting the club's cover charge.

"Get it how you live, sexy," Kee, the well-known gold digger, called out from the middle of the line.

Paulie didn't know for sure if the comment was directed at

him or not, but he turned around anyway. Kee made sure she stood out from her other two female gold-digging friends. Paulie did a double take. Not because she had hips and ass for days that had her short skirt hiked up to her smooth, thick thighs, but because Kee could be just the person to lead him to Tony. After seeing her with him in the mall, he knew she had some kind of info on him.

"Say, homie, what you need?" the hulking bouncer asked, towering over Paulie.

Paulie reached in his pocket and pulled out three stacks of new crisp bills with bank bands holding them together. He purposely flashed the stacks so Kee could see them.

"It's four of us," Paulie told him, as he peeled off four of the one-hundred-dollar bills and handed them to the bouncer while waving Kee and her other gold-digging friends over.

Paulie knew if he played his cards right, Kee would serve him Tony on a silver platter. So, he planned to splurge a little and loosen her up.

"What up, big baller? Still doing it big, I see," Kee commented as they made their way past security and headed up to the VIP section.

"Trying to, and I see you still *at it*," Paulie responded, putting emphasis on the words 'at it' to let her know he was very familiar with how she rolled.

Paulie and Kee knew each other, but didn't *'know each other'*. They ran in the same circles, knew a lot of the same people, and even sat at the same dinner table a couple times, but they never really got to know each other.

As Paulie walked through the club, he dapped up a couple hustlers from around the way. Kee and her crew watched all the love being shown to Paulie and knew without a doubt that Paulie was the man in the streets. Kee knew his rep, but that night, she saw it far exceeded her imagination. She had already conjured up a plan to get in his pockets.

"Waitress, can I get two bottles of Hen," Paulie called out over the Future song booming from the club's system.

"So, Paulie, what you got going on?" Kee asked, sitting down close to him.

"A lil' bit of this and a lil' bit of that," he replied as he felt her leg press up against his.

Paulie had seen her kind a million times over, and he was well aware of Kee's reputation of being a gold digger. He wasn't tripping about it though, because her over-the-top gold digging ways were going to make his job a whole lot easier.

Her two friends were engaged in a conversation with a couple more ballers who he recognized from South Philly. Two hours later, the two bottles were empty, and Kee was hot and obviously horny. Not a big drinker, Paulie was also feeling the effects of the Hennessey.

"What you got planned for later?" Paulie asked, rubbing his hand across her bare, oiled-up, soft thighs.

She looked down at his sparkling diamond pinky ring before answering.

"Whatever you got planned," she replied, while reaching over and rubbing her freshly manicured nails between his thighs and over his manhood.

"Well, if you're wit' what I'm thinking about, let's bounce," Paulie said, sticking to his plan on finding Tony.

Ten minutes later, they were on Catherine Street, headed to Paulie's side house.

"Nice lil' duck off spot you got here," Kee said, knowing from the overflowing mail in the box and dust on the big screen TV that he barely used this residence. She figured he had a baby mama living in his main spot out in the suburbs like all the other ballers did.

"Thanks, you want…"

Before the words were out of his mouth, Kee dropped her purse to the floor and kneeled down in front of him, pulling on his zipper. The alcohol had her on fire; she was in a real freak zone. She was no different than the rest of her crew. They all felt the quickest way into a man's pocket was by giving him some good head. Paulie just stood there looking at the freak bitch as she pulled out his semi-hard on and worked it in and out of her mouth.

"Mmm," she moaned, like his dick was dessert after a full-course meal.

After enjoying the warmth of her mouth for a minute, Paulie guided her up and led her to his bedroom.

Only seconds through the door and Paulie had her bent over the side of bed, giving it to her.

"Oh yeah, baby!" Kee called out as Paulie pounded the that ass her short skirt barely covered earlier.

All you could hear in the room was the loud smacking of thighs meeting ass and heavy moaning. Even in the coldness of the house, their bodies glistened with sweat.

"Damn, bitch! Fuck this dick! Shit!" Paulie demanded through clinched teeth.

Tightening her pussy muscles, she threw her ass to him wildly. Paulie got lost in her stride, but quickly regained his position. Not the one to be outdone, he flipped her over, lifted her legs above her head, and plowed every inch of his hardness into her, causing her to scream out in pain and pleasure. Their all-out freak session lasted for forty-five minutes. When it was over, Kee laid there trying to figure out the best way to ask Paulie for money to grab an outfit and get her hair done, while Paulie was plotting his next move to find out Tony's whereabouts so he could make him pay for Ty's murder.

They laid in each other's arms until Kee fell asleep. She was lightly snoring by the time Paulie slid out of the bed and tiptoed to the front room. He walked right over to Kee's purse that she had dropped in the middle of the floor. He unlatched it and pulled out her cell phone. Scrolling down her contact list, he softly laughed at how she had certain names labeled with tags that read "big money", "lil' money", "big dick", "shoe money", "gas money", and various other tags. He scrolled until he got to Tony's name, which was labeled "big money". He clicked on the message box and sent a blank text. Seconds later, her phone beeped, displaying a text from Tony. Paulie then began responding as if he were Kee.

Tony: what you doin'

Kee: im at the crib

Tony: you comin' thru

Kee: where am i coming to

Tony: 1022 Woodstock in North Philly take the e-way to the zoo

Kee: im coming now

After jotting down Tony's address, he cleared the messages, crept back into the room, and got in the bed.

* * * * *

The next night, Paulie rode down Girard Avenue in the tinted-out, black minivan headed to Woodstock Street. The van blended in perfectly with the murky streets. Paulie rode slouched in the seat, with his black hoodie pulled low and the .44 automatic in his lap. He found the address easily. After checking the scene, he found a parking space a few houses up from the address. He could tell Tony wasn't in the house, so he slid down in his seat and waited patiently to see if he would show up soon.

"Fuck this nigga at?" he spat out loud, after sitting and watching the house for almost an hour.

Just as he was about to abort his mission, he saw two headlights slowly coming in his direction. The BMW 750i, the same kind and color Ty had, lucked up on a spot right in front of his door.

Paulie didn't waste any time. He was out the van before Tony could kill the engine of the BMW. He ducked low with the .44 in his grip and bag on his shoulder. Tony was too gone off the numerous shots of tequila he just had at the bar to even notice the dark figure crouched down low and heading in his direction.

Paulie checked the scene and saw that he was alone. He held the .44 so tight that the veins were popping out the back of his hand. He pushed up on the driver's side, lifted up, and stuck the .44 automatic through the window.

"Yeah, what's popping, lil' nigga?" Paulie said coolly, as he pulled the hoodie from his head so Tony could see him clearly.

Tony's eyes got big as golf balls, and just as he was about to reach for his Glock, he remembered he had tucked it in the glove compartment. He knew he didn't stand a chance of getting to it.

"Ah, Paulie, what up my—"

"That's yo ass, boy. Oh, and by the way, do you still need the work you hit me for?" Paulie asked sarcastically, as he grabbed the bag containing four and a half of raw from his shoulder and tossed it through the window into his lap.

Tony looked up confused, but then it hit him. He knew then he was a dead man.

"Man, Paulie, wh—"

The boom from the .44 pierced Paulie's ears while it silenced Tony. The first shot hit him in the neck, rocking him sideways.

Pop! Pop!

The next two shots caught him as he raised back up. The hollow points tore through his skull with ease. His whole head exploded, sending brain matter all over the dashboard and windshield. He slumped forward in his seat with most of his head gone.

Paulie pulled his hoodie back over his head and slowly walked to his van.

"'Cuz, I got you," he said as he brought the van's engine to life and put it in drive.

G STREET CHRONICLES
~A NEW URBAN DYNASTY~

WWW.GSTREETCHRONICLES.COM

TONYSTORY

CHAPTER 12

G STREET CHRONICLES
~A NEW URBAN DYNASTY~

WWW.GSTREETCHRONICLES.COM

"This is getting out of hand. When is it going to ever stop?" Detective Kim Ritz said with disgust in her tone.

She stood behind Detective Johansen, who was the lead detective on the scene, as he went through the pockets of the murder victim, whose body was slumped over in the car.

"Yeah, it's getting really bad out here," Johansen said, already knowing the identity of the man who lay dead before him.

"This city is like a fuckin' war zone, and it ain't getting no better. I'm going to ask around and see if anybody saw or heard anything. You need me for anything else here?" Ritz asked, tucking her hands in her pockets while her eyes remained on the gruesome sight of Tony's head that was practically blown off.

"Nah, I'm fine. Just see if you can find us some witnesses," Johansen told her, as he continued his inspection of the dead man's body.

"Alright, I'll be just a call away," she said, peering over him once more to look at the bullet-riddled body in the car.

"Okay."

In deep thought, Johansen stood up and watched the other investigators and police mark the scene of the crime. He walked over to his car and pulled his cell phone out of his pocket. After dialing a number, he let it ring until the voicemail picked up.

"Get back with me ASAP," he said, then took a deep breath and clicked off the line.

He leaned up against his unmarked car looking up in the air, but was jarred out of his thoughts by an up and coming rookie detective.

"Sir, we found all the shell casings and marked the locations. Looks like a .44 cal did the job," the young freckle-faced detective said with excitement, as if he had already solved the case.

"Good job, Jimmy. Make sure you get this processed too. Looks like cocaine. We'll know for sure when it gets back from the lab. Look, whatever you find here, make sure you report it directly to me. You understand?" Johansen said with firmness in his tone.

"I understand, sir," Jimmy said, then saluted the detective and went back to canvassing the scene.

Johansen hid his anger well. He was frustrated and wanted answers.

TONYSTORY

CHAPTER 13

THREE WEEKS LATER

G STREET CHRONICLES
~A NEW URBAN DYNASTY~

WWW.GSTREETCHRONICLES.COM

"The next three rounds are on me!" Paulie called out from the Luxe Lounge VIP section that he shared with his old partner, Nasir, from South Philly and three of the baddest females in the spot.

Paulie's drought was over. Since Tony had been eliminated from the scene, his work was moving non-stop. His workers were back flooding the city, and the money was stacking two-fold. Lately, Paulie had been hitting the different nightspots around the city more than usual. He had gone from being laidback and low key, to flashy and the life of the party.

"Man, we need to link up and put something on the table. I know we can set the city on fire," Nasir said, sipping on his third Henny and Coke while balancing one of the females on his lap, who moved and gyrated to the Chief Keef blasting from the club's sound system.

"Nigga, you don't see the smoke? I already got this shit on fire, but we can see about New York and New Jersey. Them niggas doing they thang up there, but they still looking to be touched like a virgin bitch," Paulie said boastfully, as the two girls on each side of him took down round after round.

"That's all gangsta, too, but enough about that. Let's entertain," Nasir said, cutting the conversation, knowing they were breaking the rules of the street by talking in front of the girls.

"I'm wit' that," Paulie said, turning his attention to the two girls who were now highly intoxicated and dancing in their seats.

The whole time, Monk and Quadir sat back watching Paulie put on and show off for the women. The streets were talking about Tony's murder and Paulie's possible involvement. Word traveled fast and niggas from all over Philly were listening, even Tony's loyal partners.

"LB said he used the bitch Kee to set Tony up," Monk told Quadir, who was dumb to the facts.

"Kee? The fine-ass bitch from Johnson Homes?" Quadir asked, remembering Kee from his old block.

"Yeah, that's the one. Ma breaking these lame-ass niggas around here. LB said he found his brother's cell phone in his spot and checked it out. He saw a couple texts from Kee telling Tony she wanted to come through. He gave her the address to his spot, and that has to be how that nigga pulled up on him," Monk said with venom in his tone and a frown on his face as he watched Paulie down another drink.

"Word?" Quadir barked, knowing Kee had gotten herself in deep trouble with the wrong dudes.

"Yeah, she set the homie up for the nigga Paulie," Monk emphasized.

"How y'all figure it was Paulie, though?" Quadir inquired.

"Just before he got killed, word around was that Paulie was gunning for Tony for the murder of his cousin Ty. Damn, nigga, you ain't heard?" Monk said, while watching Paulie pull out a stack of money and heavily tip the waitress.

"Man, you know I've been ducked low since that J-Rock lick," Quadir explained.

"We'll lean back for a minute and wait for him to bounce," Monk instructed, as they sat in the far corner of the club and continued to watch Paulie's every move.

* * * * *

On the west side of town on Lansdowne Avenue, LB and Mikey were strapped and rounding the back of Kee's two-bedroom home.

"Say, my nig, I told you I could most likely jimmy this one," Mikey told LB, then tucked his burner in his waist and pulled the screwdriver from his back pocket.

The night's cold wind whistled as he jammed the screwdriver in the edge of the door and popped it open.

"Bingo," LB said through the ski mask he had pulled down over his face.

They slowly pushed the back door open and entered.

* * * * *

"The nigga's 'bout to bounce," Quadir told Monk as he stood up from the bar stool, making sure he didn't lose Paulie in the crowded club.

"Let's go lay on 'em," Monk said, downing the remaining gin and juice in his glass, then following Quadir out front.

As Paulie and Nasir walked through the crowd, hustlers, dope boys, pimps, and other major players dapped them up like they were celebrities. Both men were definitely known in the city, but being with Paulie that night had boosted Nasir's street celebrity status, and he picked up on it instantly.

"Y'all ride with Nasir, and I'll meet y'all at the Hyatt in thirty minutes. I gotta make a stop," Paulie told them, then turned and headed in the opposite direction to the club's side exit door.

Paulie was a vet in the streets, so he knew how to stay one step ahead of the game. That's why he had parked next to the side exit.

"A'ight," Nasir told him before ushering the ladies out the front door and into his customized, tinted-out Cadillac Escalade.

By the time Monk and Quadir, who were crouched down in Monk's old Delta '88, had spotted them, the trio was climbing in Nasir's truck.

"There they go," Quadir said as he reached around and grabbed the six-shot pump from the backseat.

* * * * *

The house was dark, quiet, and sparsely furnished. LB and Mikey eased through the front room quietly in search of Kee. A minute later, they were in the hallway leading back to her master bedroom.

"Check that room," LB whispered to Mikey as they passed a closed door.

Mikey quietly pushed the room door open and saw that it was an unoccupied guest room. He quickly retreated and caught up to LB, who was easing through Kee's master bedroom door. Both men readied their guns as they stepped in the room and made their way over to the bed where Kee was sound asleep.

"Psst! Psst!" LB sounded off, as he took the barrel of his gun and used it to move the covers back from her face.

Mikey stood on the opposite side of the bed with his long-nose .357 aimed at Kee, who was now waking up from her deep sleep.

* * * * *

Quadir and Monk waited until the Escalade pulled out of the lot before pulling out from their parking spot. They trailed the Escalade through the Philly late-night traffic as it exceeded the speed limit.

"That nigga got to be DUI the way he swerving. Look, as soon as he turns off of Market Street, we gonna pull up on him at the first stop sign," Monk said, as the Escalade made a right like he'd hoped.

"Just pull up next to him so I can get a good jump o—"

Honk! Honk!

A car horn cut Quadir off mid-sentence. A sleek Maserati pulled around them in the right lane, signaling for the Escalade to stop. Monk and Quadir fell back and watched the exchange. That's when they realized the man in the Maserati was Paulie.

"The nigga ain't in the truck!" Quadir said, while reaching for the door handle of the Delta '88.

Before he could get the door open, Paulie was speeding off through the city's back streets. Monk hit the gas, trying to be as discreet as possible while chasing him down. Paulie never noticed the men following him as he entered the expressway. Monk and Quadir turned onto the expressway behind him, but soon realized the Delta '88 couldn't keep up with the turbo-charged

Maserati. The Maserati lingered along for a few minutes, then took off in the distance.

"Fuck!" Monk spat as the car disappeared.

* * * * *

"Wh…who…ahhh!" Kee screamed, but it didn't last long after the butt of LB's Glock .40 connected with her mouth, silencing her.

Blood spewed from her mouth and onto her cream-colored Chanel comforter.

"Bitch, shut the fuck up!" LB snapped as he reached over, grabbed her by her expensive Brazilian weave, and snatched her out of bed.

Mikey's manhood slightly rose at the sight of the thick, perfectly-built Kee wearing nothing but thongs and a tank top.

"Please, don't hurt me! Please!" Kee cried out from the floor, while holding her busted lips that were leaking blood.

"Oh, so it's 'please don't hurt me' now, huh? When you was setting my brother up, it was all good, fuck-ass hoe!" LB reared back and smacked Kee sideways.

"Ahhh! Set up? I swear I ain't set nobody up! I don't know what you're talking 'bout!" Kee spat nervously.

"So you don't know what I'm talking about?" LB said, standing over her with his pistol in her face while she looked up at him with pitiful eyes.

Kee had been around the streets and knew the men who now stood in her spot planned on killing her before they left. The fact that they wore no masks helped her come up with that assumption. She was sure they planned on leaving no witnesses.

"Please tell me what's going on! What is this all about? I swear I don't know what y'all talking 'bout!" Kee pleaded as tears ran down her cheeks.

"Bitch, what's this?" LB screamed.

He reached in his pocket, pulled Tony's cell phone out, and shoved it in her face. Kee looked at the screen but still didn't realize what was going on.

"I...I don't understand. What are you saying?" Kee asked nervously as she stared at the cell phone LB held.

LB reached down, grabbed a hand full of her weave, snatched her up off the floor, and slammed her down in the computer desk chair in the bedroom.

"Owww!" she screamed out.

LB stuck the phone back in her face. "Look right here! Remember these? Bitch, you texted my brother and asked for his address. Look, bitch!" LB's hand slightly shook while holding the phone in place.

"I didn't text yo—" Kee started, then stopped to look at the date of the text.

She remembered the night in question. It was her girl Tootsie's birthday, the same night she left the club with Paulie.

"Oh no! Please, those texts are not from me! I swear they ain't!" Kee cried.

She thought back on the night with Paulie, knowing he must have used her phone to text Tony.

"You set my brother up for that fuck-nigga Paulie, and now, bitch, we gonna make you feel it." LB glanced over at his right-hand man Mikey, who stood watching quietly but ready for whatever.

"Help! No! Helllllp!" Kee screamed at the top of her lungs.

Mikey retrieved the roll of duct tape from his jacket pocket and proceeded to tape her to the computer chair.

"Hoe, you set up the wrong nigga this time," LB barked, hitting her in the mouth and silencing her again.

Mikey overpowered Kee as she fought against his attempts to tape her in the chair.

"I swear I didn't text him. It was Paulie! It had to have been him, 'cause he was the one with me the whole night!" Kee said with a strong slur.

Putting it all together, she realized Paulie had used her.

"Whatever. All y'all gold-digging bitches are just alike!" Mikey said as he plugged in the iron that was on the ironing board.

"Yeah, bitch, ain't no fun now, is it? Shit!" LB covered her mouth with tape, then touched the bottom of the iron to see if it was hot.

Kee sat taped to the chair with a blood-matted face and disheveled hair. She wiggled and kicked violently trying to get loose, but knew it was all in vain.

"Ummm!" Kee screamed from under the tape as the hot iron was placed on her smooth thigh.

Mikey smiled while resting the hot iron on other parts of her body. The men took turns burning Kee while watching her squirm and squeal. After fifteen minutes of torture, LB pulled his .40 Glock from his waist, removed the tape that had kept her silent, and jammed the gun in her mouth.

"Fuck-ass bitch!" LB called out, then pulled the trigger.

The blast blew through Kee's mouth and head, killing her instantly.

Despite being a killer, Mikey flinched at the sight of the once beautiful face of Kee that was now disfigured and mangled by the hollow point from the Glock.

"Let's go!" Mikey said, as LB tucked the gun in his waist and stepped over the gruesome sight.

TONY STORY

CHAPTER 14

G STREET CHRONICLES
~A NEW URBAN DYNASTY~

WWW.GSTREETCHRONICLES.COM

The next day, all of North Philly was talking about Kee's murder. LB's circle was leaking the word out, and by noon, the word had reached Paulie.

"Tony's brother…the lil' wild nigga, right?" Paulie asked. He sought confirmation from Keith, one of his trusted street connects, after receiving the call.

"Yeah, he gunning for you. So, stay ahead of the game," Keith told him. The sound of urgency in his voice let Paulie know this news was not to be taken lightly. "Word is that he the one that bodied Kee, talking 'bout she helped you by settin' up Tony. Niggas and bitches talking about some kind of text you sent or some shit, but, bruh, get right. Shit 'bout to hit the fan," Keith warned, alerting his good friend of the opposing danger.

"Nigga, you know I stay right. Appreciate the heads up though," Paulie replied, thinking of his next move.

"Just stay safe, my man. I'll be in touch," Keith said, ending the call.

Paulie scrolled down his contact list looking for Trell's number.

Trell was one of his associates who could help him reach Killa and Stu, two of the most dangerous killers to ever walk the streets of Philly.

Paulie listened as the Scarface ringback tone played in his ear. "Yo?"

"What up, fam?" Paulie said, greeting his old friend.

"Boy, what it do! Nigga, you been the talk of the streets. I had to tell this one young nigga to shut up about it, 'cause the more talk, the better chance it has getting to the suits. These niggas don't understand what dry snitching is. What's the deal with you, man?" Trell asked, knowing Paulie was deep in a street war.

"Yeah, shit been thick on this end. I need to get in touch with Killa and Stu," Paulie said. He knew Trell would pick up on his intentions without him having to say anything more.

"Oh, okay. You know I keep them two niggas on speed dial. I'll hit 'em and have 'em hit you up," he replied.

"Do that my nigga. I'll holla," Paulie said, knowing the two killers would handle LB for a reasonable price.

Ten minutes after hanging up with Trell, Paulie's phone vibrated.

"Hello?"

"You checking for us?" Killa asked. He and his partner Stu were sitting out in the backyard of their shabby, broken-down row house playing with KO, their red nose pit bull.

"Yeah, I need to see if you still doing construction work." Paulie spoke in code, but was certain Killa would pick up on his request.

Killa laughed as Stu slapped KO around, making him growl and snap at him.

"I ain't never going to retire my hammer. What you need done?" Killa asked, while reaching over to grab the Newport Stu had been smoking and pulled on it hard.

"I'm going to be at Delilah's at two o'clock. I'll holla at you then," Paulie told him, then disconnected the call.

Killa pressed the End button, reared back in the old folding chair, and rubbed his goatee before he spoke.

"Yo, bro, we got work," he said, blowing out smoke that hovered in the air like a cloud of fog.

"Right on time, 'cause my money looking real funny," Stu said, as he kneeled down in front of KO and continued slapping him around.

Stu was older, less spoken, and the deadlier of the two. He was thirty-two, a few years older than his partner in crime, dark skin, wore a close cut, always clean shaven, thin, and looked completely harmless. The two men linked up back when they were teenagers and committed a liquor store robbery. Killa got caught, while Stu fled the scene. The police pulled every trick in the book to get Killa to talk and give up his accomplice, but he stayed solid and kept his mouth closed. He took his five-year bid upstate like a true soldier, never mumbling a word to the suits. Stu didn't know how his young partner was going to roll when the pressure hit, but after the dust cleared and Killa was shipped off to prison, he knew his friend, his partner, his nigga had stood solid on his behalf.

The two had been similar in size and color, but that changed while Killa was away. The dark-skinned man came home with a muscular body, bald head, goatee, and unfortunately, now walked with a limp. The leg injury was caused by the intense type of treatment he endured during questioning when he wouldn't give up information on Stu.

As soon as Killa came home, they were back at it, but this time, Stu introduced him to a more profitable profession… murder for hire. Although known around the city for their murderous ways, they always managed to elude the law. They only took jobs from two people: Squire, an old-school hustler from 18th Street, and Trell, Killa's nephew.

Paulie sat in his Maserati on the side of Delilah's waiting on Killa and Stu to show. When he saw the dusty, green, late-model Cadillac pull in and park off in the corner of the lot, he knew it had to be them. Paulie waved his hand out the window, signaling for them to come over to his car. The two men and Paulie had done business in the past. However, before the men could take out the man that Paulie had contracted them to kill, he was busted by the Feds and hauled off to federal prison, leaving Paulie extremely dissatisfied with their no-refund policy.

Dressed in black jeans and hoodies, Killa and Stu walked casually across the lot. Paulie reached over and pushed open the passenger door to his Maserati. Stu climbed in the front, while Killa opened the back door and slid in the backseat.

"Who's the nigga and what you paying?" Stu asked, getting straight to the point while Killa sat quietly waiting for the details.

Paulie looked over at Stu, then glanced in his rearview mirror at Killa before he spoke.

"Nigga's name is LB, Tony's younger brother. Lil' nigga been talking reckless like he trying to see me on some gunplay shit. I need him taken care of, and it's worth twenty-five thousand dollars to me," Paulie said, putting a price on his own lick. Again, he looked over at Stu, who he knew was the shot caller of the two.

Stu turned in his seat and looked back at Killa, who slowly ran his hand down his goatee and then nodded his head in agreement.

"Deal. I know the young nigga. He run with Dino and KenRaw. We got you, but money up front," Stu informed him.

Paulie pulled two envelopes from under his seat.

"I know the deal," Paulie said, handing Stu the two envelopes.

Stu, in turn, handed them to Killa in the backseat.

The men sat in silence as Killa counted the money.

"All good," Killa confirmed once he finished.

They opened the car doors and climbed out.

"We'll be in touch," Stu told him before closing the door and walking away.

* * * * *

LB made a left on 10th and Thompson in his old-school Pontiac and jumped out at the corner store a block from his spot. The Lean had him walking sideways and feeling on top of the world. He stepped in the store, purchased a box of Swishers, and headed back to the car, ready to roll up a fat spliff of the Kush he had just bought from 13th Street. Just as he opened his car door, shots rang out.

Pop! Pop! Pop!

The bullets pierced the Pontiac's metal, quickly changing the flawless body of the car. LB quickly dropped behind his car's rear fender and pulled his strap, ready to return fire. Cocking his .9mm, he rounded the car prepared to bust back. He tried his best to get up on whoever the shooters were lurking in the corner store's shadows. Just as he leveled in on one of the dark figures firing from the darkness, his gun misfired.

"Fuck!" he barked as he cocked the gun again, trying to free the bullet stuck in the chamber.

After readying his gun for a second time, he rose up and pulled the trigger. The gun blasts lit up the parking lot, sending people scurrying for cover. He kept busting back as he fled the scene, and out of nowhere, he heard a cry in the distance. LB didn't know where the cry came from or who it was, but he didn't bother trying to find out.

In the parking lot, Killa lay struggling to take his last breath. LB didn't realize he'd hit Killa with a wild shot. The .9mm hollow point pierced his neck, sending him to the ground. Stu knew it was no use hanging around trying to save his friend who had blood squirting from his neck, so he turned and retreated into the darkness.

* * * * *

LB hit the alley full speed, praying he wasn't hit from behind while trying to get away. After getting to a safe spot, he stopped to catch his breath.

"Fuck! It's on now!" he screamed as he tore open the Swisher package and fished around in his pocket for his lighter.

Before lighting his Swisher, he checked the chamber on his .9mm and readied the gun. He then pulled on the Swisher, wishing it was filled with the loud Kush tucked away in the glove compartment of his Pontiac. He knew Paulie was behind the attack, and he declared retaliation to the fullest.

After sitting in the alley for close to two hours, LB stepped out and headed back to the corner store. The last of the police were pulling out of the lot when he walked up. Just as he reached his car, a Crown Vic pulled in next to his car. He cursed himself for returning to the scene strapped with his burner.

Detective Johansen threw his door open and jumped out of the unmarked car with his badge in plain view.

"Excuse me, sir. Can I speak with you for a minute?" he asked, while giving LB a thorough inspection.

"What up? What you wanna talk to me about?" LB snapped, looking Johansen up and down.

"I need to talk to you about the shots you fired that killed a man out here," Johansen said, pointing in the direction where Killa was found dead.

"Man, I don't know what the hell you talking 'bout." LB turned, opened his car door, and climbed in.

Johansen grabbed the car door by the side hinge and stepped in front of it before LB could pull it closed.

"Look you, I know what the fuck been going on out here in these streets, so just between me and you...let it go. Get out of town, out of sight. Let shit die down. Feel me?" Johansen said, then released the door and stepped aside.

He hoped LB took heed, because the city was in an uproar, which made it hard for money to be made. And that wasn't a good thing.

LB just looked up at the detective and slammed his car door shut.

"Disappear," Johansen said right before LB turned up his powerful sound system.

All that could be heard as he pulled off was the loud duals and rattling from the trunk where the twelve-inch speakers were housed.

LB digested the detective's words as he turned onto Hutchinson Street, then made a quick left on 9th Street. He knew he could chill for a minute in his old hood. He needed time to clear his head, to zone out for a minute. Pulling over to the curb, he turned on his interior light, popped the glove box, and grabbed the bag of Kush. Pulling a Swisher from his pocket, he opened it and squeezed it until the tobacco loosened. After loosening up the tobacco, he dumped it out and stuffed the Swisher with the funny-textured loud weed.

"Damn!" he seethed as he reached down to pick up his cup of Lean that had tipped over and stained the custom, smoke-grey floor mat.

Firing up the blunt, LB thought about what had just transpired. He knew he was a marked man, but didn't give a fuck. He also knew Paulie was the puppet master working the strings. Paulie had killed Tony, his big brother, and now LB was going to make him pay.

LB pulled on the Swisher, inhaling deep. He was pissed and didn't care if he lived or died; he didn't give a fuck. He pulled the .9mm from his waist and ejected the clip. Laying the blunt in the ashtray, he fished around under the seat for the box of bullets. With a "fuck the world" attitude, he loaded sixteen of them in the clip and one in the chamber.

Tap! Tap! Tap!

Loud tapping on his passenger side window made him jump, almost letting off a couple of rounds at Mikey.

"Nigga! Man, you almost caught a hot one," LB said, lowering the gun.

Mikey opened the car door and got in.

"Bro! What the hell you doing out here parked all up on the

curb? You know the boys been patrolling around here hard," Mikey said, reaching for the simmering blunt in the ashtray.

"Fuck the pigs, homie! Niggas just let loose on me up at the corner store. Nigga, you know it's fuckin' on now," LB barked, feeling every muscle in his body slowly relaxing from the effects of the blunt.

"Nigga drew heat on you? What nigga done made a death wish?" Mikey asked, pulling on the blunt until the tip lit up bright red.

"'Cuz, I don't know the gunners, but I know that bitch-nigga Paulie got something to do with it. His ass is mine, ya hear me!" LB fumed, reaching for the blunt.

"Paulie? This shit 'bout that Ty situation, huh? Oh, the bitch Kee, too?" Mikey asked, putting it all together.

"Lights out for these bitches, my nigga!" LB exploded, then pulled on the blunt hard and held the smoke in until it made him cough.

"Nigga, you know how I roll. I fucks with you and Tony the long way," Mikey told him, reaching in his pants and pulling out his Colt .357.

"Nigga, you know what it is," LB said, cracking the window and flicking the roach outside.

TONYSTORY

CHAPTER 15

G STREET CHRONICLES
~A NEW URBAN DYNASTY~

WWW.GSTREETCHRONICLES.COM

The next day, Paulie sat on the edge of his bed holding the phone, pissed off and rubbing his head as Stu gave him the details of the failed attempt on LB.

"Come on, man, I paid y'all extra to handle this nigga, and now you sitting here telling me that he still walking the streets!" Paulie huffed.

He stood up and started pacing back and forth in the expensively furnished, spacious room.

"We had the nigga cornered, but luck was on the nigga side, straight up. Killa most likely didn't make it, my nigga. I ain't heard shit yet. We had the drop on this nigga. Then he ducked off and started busting back. Fam, I got this nigga. I got this nigga for real, man," Stu said uneasily, as he reflected back on his right-hand man lying in a pool of blood, screaming and holding his neck while blood oozed through his fingers.

"I wanted this nigga by Sunday. I ain't got time for you to have this nigga! So what you telling me is to be a sitting duck for this young fuck nigga until you catch up with him! Yeah, whatever.

Bet'cha I don't get no hot ones slippin'. I'll get at you," Paulie said.

After hanging up, he entered his walk-in closet, which housed no less than one hundred sneaker boxes.

Paulie wasn't going to wait around for Stu to handle the young nigga. He grabbed the canvas bag from the corner and fished around inside it until his hand rested on his chrome Desert Eagle. He pulled out the gun, then reached back in the bag and grabbed two extra clips, both full.

"I'll just handle this lil' nigga myself," Paulie mumbled to himself, as he pulled his all-black Dickie suit and black Nikes out the closet.

After getting dressed, he called Exquisite Hair, his girl Deja's salon. She was pushing his new black-on-black Charger.

The receptionist walked over and handed Deja the cordless phone, letting her know it was Paulie.

"Hey, babe. What's up?" Deja answered.

"Baby, I need you to come through and switch cars with me before you head back out to your mom's. Did the people I sent ever come through and fix your tire?" he asked, planning to wait on nightfall to make his move.

"No. They said tomorrow. They really pissing me off now," she fussed. "Alright, I'll be there, but you'll have to give me a minute. I have a late appointment," she explained, while flat-ironing one of her customer's hair.

"I'll get back with them and handle it. Alright, boo, I'll see you when you get here," Paulie said.

He contemplated driving to the salon himself, but decided to wait for her since he wasn't in a hurry.

Then he thought about just driving the Maserati. What he really needed was his Kevlar vest, and it was in the trunk of the

Charger. So, he decided to chill and handle some business while waiting for Deja.

* * * * *

Later that evening, after finishing up her last appointment, Deja stepped out of the shop and locked up. The sun had disappeared behind the horizon, and the moon was suddenly appearing. Deja cruised down Ogontz Avenue behind the Charger's dark tint, heading to Paulie's spot. While cruising, she toyed with the Charger's high-powered motor modifications Paulie had installed that made the car go from 0 to 60 miles per hour in seconds. As soon as she made a right on Broad Street, a dented-up old Chevy made a right behind her. LB sat dipped low behind the wheel with a Philly baseball cap pulled down low over his eyes. Deja was completely unaware of the danger that lurked behind her in the old Chevy.

"Yeah, I got this nigga's ass now! Let's get this nigga!" Mikey called out from the passenger seat, his Colt resting in his lap.

"We'll catch the nigga at the next light," LB said as he reached down, pulled his .9mm from his waist, and laid it on the seat between them.

It seemed like it took forever to get to the next light. Gone off the Kush and Ciroc, LB and Mikey were ready to wreak havoc on Paulie and anybody rolling with him.

"Get ready, nigga," LB said, while peering through his rearview mirror to make sure the coast was clear.

"Nigga, I'm on it!" Mikey barked as he picked up the Colt from his lap and gripped it tight.

Stopping at the light, Deja bobbed her head to the new

Keisha Cole CD.

"Let's get it!" LB screamed, then threw the car in park and jumped out.

Mikey was two steps ahead of him with his Colt extended, ready to blast. Deja waited patiently for the light to change, unaware of the two men approaching from behind. Just as they got up on the Charger, the light changed and Deja mashed the gas. Before she could pull off, gunshots rang out.

Pop! Boom! Pop! Pop! Boom!

Deja's foot pressed down even heavier on the pedal as the window of the Charger shattered. Bullets pierced the interior of the car, tearing through the metal, fiberglass, and leather. Two shots hit Deja, who was now racing through the back streets recklessly in an attempt to get away.

"Ahhh!" she screamed, crying as she held her arm close to her side.

She was lucky that Mikey's shots missed her and LB's two connecting shots weren't fatal. She raced away from the danger, barely avoiding a head-on collision with a van. She was so scared that she didn't realize she had crossed the yellow line and the van was coming directly at her. Startled by the blowing of horns, she snapped back just in time to swerve the Charger over into her lane. With her adrenalin still pumping, she ran right through an intersection, carelessly slamming into the side of an SUV whose driver clearly had the right of way.

The Charger's fiberglass crumbled easily upon impact. Deja's head hit the windshield, knocking her out cold. Drivers slammed on their brakes, attempting to avoid the collision. People were throwing their cars in park and jumping out to render aide to the drivers of the two cars. While not injured, the man behind the wheel of the Cadillac Escalade was shaken up pretty bad. Cell phone lights lit up the street as the motorists standing by took videos of the scene.

Within minutes, police and other emergency vehicles had swarmed the scene. The EMT's and police were confused at first, seeing that Deja's wounds weren't consistent with the accident. After conferring and going over the scene again, they realized the unconscious woman had been shot and had most likely fled the scene of the attack.

Medics removed Deja from the mangled car and rushed her to Einstein Hospital's emergency room.

* * * * *

"Yeah, nigga!" Mikey called out, while jumping back in the passenger seat of the Chevy.

"That's what a nigga get for fucking with the LB!" LB screamed as he threw the car in drive and sped off in the opposite direction.

"Yeah, body niggas!" Mikey added, tucking his burner in his waist.

"Man, that nigga can't still be breathing! I know I unloaded this whole clip on his ass," LB said, reaching under his seat for the plastic bag filled with weed.

"I let all six of mine go, and my cannon don't play," Mikey said with emphasis. He reached over, grabbed the bag from LB, and looked for the Swishers on the seat between them.

"Nigga probably taking his last breath right now. Roll up a fat one, nigga. I want to get blowed. What ya pockets looking like?" LB asked as he made his way back to their old hood.

"Nigga, ain't shit changed since the last time I told you. I'm fucked up. Boy, I need a quick come up," Mikey told him. As they cruised the back streets, he emptied the tobacco from the Swisher out the car window.

"Let's pay a nigga a visit. I know just the person," LB said menacingly.

"Let's make it do what it do," Mikey agreed, while looking for the extra bullets he brought for the Colt.

TONY STORY

CHAPTER 16

G STREET CHRONICLES
~A NEW URBAN DYNASTY~

WWW.GSTREETCHRONICLES.COM

The longer it took Deja to arrive, the madder Paulie got. When she didn't answer the shop phone or her cell phone, he grew even madder. He dozed off while waiting for her, and the ringing of his cell phone awakened him.

"Hello?" he snapped, not recognizing the number on the screen.

"Paulie Sims?" the voice on the other end of the phone questioned.

"Who is this?" Paulie asked roughly. Regardless of how sexy the voice sounded, he did not reveal himself to the caller who referred to him by his first and last name.

"My name is Kim Ritz. I'm calling to inform you that your friend, Deja Williams, was in an accident in your car. She's at Einstein in ICU." Detective Ritz purposely held back the information of the shooting.

"Deja? I'll be right there!"

He hung up the phone and rushed out the door, forgetting about his plan and forgetting about LB for the moment.

Paulie didn't waste any time getting to the hospital. He arrived within fifteen minutes, found a parking spot, and ran into the hospital, where he aggressively asked the receptionist for directions to the ICU. When he stepped off the elevator and walked toward the ICU, he noticed an officer standing by one of the rooms. Being in the presence of cops made anybody from Paulie's lifestyle uneasy, but right then, Paulie concerned himself more with finding Deja. That is, until the nurse informed him that was Deja's room the officer was standing guard in front of.

What the hell is going on? Why is the police in front of her room? What the hell happened? Paulie wondered as he walked toward the room.

"Hi and you are?" the officer standing outside of Deja's room questioned Paulie, blocking him from entering the room.

"I'm Paulie Sims. Your people called and told me that my lady was in an accident. Now could you excuse me," Paulie said, trying to bypass the officer.

The officer stood firm in position.

"Could you step over here with me for a second, sir?" the officer said, following the orders that were given to him.

"What's the problem? Is she—" Paulie started.

"Oh, no. She's going to be okay. My superior just has a couple of questions for you before you go in to see her," the officer told Paulie, then grabbed his radio off his side and spoke a code into it.

Not even a minute later, two people exited the room: a female who stopped by the officer's side and Detective Johansen. Paulie's eyes registered surprise at the sight of Johansen, not expecting to see him there and especially coming out of Deja's room.

"Hi, Tommy. I appreciate you and Detective Ritz calling me.

I'll take it from here," Johansen said, pausing to make sure they were out of earshot.

Paulie leaned back on the wall, crossed his arms over his chest, and looked at Johansen. *What the fuck is he doing here?* Paulie wanted to ask him, but kept his thoughts to himself.

"Look, Paulie, I warned you about all of this shit. I told you what was going to happen if you carried out the shit with Tony. Now look at this shit. It's out of fuckin' control! Wink is leaning on me to make sure his product moves in the street smoothly, and I'm depending on you. But, you running around with this cowboy bullshit, fucking up the bigger picture."

"Look, man—"

"Shut the fuck up and listen! I covered for your ass for the last time! You fuckin' killed Tony and left an assload of evidence that I had to sweep up under the rug. Fuckin' fingerprints on shell casings and a fuckin' leather bag of dope that had enough of your DNA on it for your ass to pass Go and go straight to jail! Look, if we going to keep doing business, you need to put that gun down and get back to what really counts...makin' fuckin' money. Your girl is in there right now with bullet holes in her because of this shit. She—"

"What!" Paulie yelled and tried to move past Johansen to go to Deja's side, but was blocked.

"I'm not finished. She slammed into another vehicle while fleeing from somebody trying to kill her. But, I'm sure whoever did this thought it was you in that car and not her. You need to chill out, because it's getting harder and harder to cover for your ass. I got Wink dropping thirty tomorrow at the warehouse that needs to be moved fast. So, fuck all of this retaliation shit and let's get back to work. Ty is dead and gone; Tony is dead and gone. Shit's even now," Johansen fumed. When he looked up, he saw an old friend approaching them.

"Detective!" the veteran officer and investigator called out as he marched down the hall of the hospital.

"Carter Winslow, how's it going?" Johansen asked, stepping away from Paulie and walking over to his old police friend who did occasional investigations for the department.

"Look, I know you're here on official business, but I need to speak with you for a few minutes. It's very important. Got something to show you."

The two were close enough to Paulie for him to hear them loud and clear.

Waiting to finish up his conversation with Johansen, Paulie turned his back on the men as if he wasn't interested in their conversation. He really wanted to rush into the room to see Deja, but at the same time, he wanted to know what this little made-to-look like a surprise visit was all about.

"What you got for me, Carter?" Johansen asked, curious about the information his old friend was about to pass along.

"Look, you know I've been in on all the murders since day one, and—"

"Hold up. What murders, Carter? Slow down," Johansen said, stopping him mid-sentence.

"Okay. Just kind of excited right now." Carter took a deep breath before resuming. "The killings on the north side...you know the guy Ty and then the other guy Tony that was killed in his car. Well, I did a thorough investigation on everything collected at both scenes. I had little to go on at the scene with the guy Ty, but what I do know is that Tony was there and now he's dead. The second murder at the car is a different story. A lot of the evidence was tainted, but as you know, I make sure I collect my own when I can. It just so happens that I recovered a shell casing that contained a fingerprint," Carter explained, peaking Johansen's and Paulie's interest.

"Shell casing?" Johansen asked.

"Yeah, I took one from the scene to examine it, and I'm glad I did. This is the guy we need to find," Carter said, while pulling a small piece of paper from his pocket.

Paulie turned just as Carter handed Johansen the paper that contained a name. Johansen's face turned beet red as he looked at the name Paulie Sims scribbled on the paper. He was furious that his old friend was still up to his renegade ways of investigating cases that he had no business investigating.

"You sure about this Paulie Sims, Carter?" Johansen purposely spoke loud enough for Paulie to hear.

Paulie dropped his head at the mention of his name and crept off, bypassing Deja's room.

"Positive as a whore's STD test," Carter stated with confidence.

"Who else knows about this?" Johansen asked, reaching out and resting his hand on his old friend's shoulder while looking him straight in his eyes.

"Nobody but me, and you now. I got enough evidence now to present this to the top brass. I'll show them that looking over me for detective was a big mistake. Shit, this just may be the break I need to earn the position. What you think?" Carter asked with excitement in his tone. He knew bringing a killer to justice would be a good look on his resume.

Johansen lowered his voice to slightly above a whisper. "Yeah, you right, but let me help you. I want to see exactly what you got…everything. After both of us assess everything, we'll determine an angle. I'll even help you by giving you the intel I have concerning the investigation, which we both know is totally against policy. So, you're going to have to keep it quiet. I can trust you, right?"

Johansen scanned the area to make sure no one was around. He knew he had to put out the fire that Carter was about to pour gas on.

* * * * *

Paulie exited the hospital, frequently looking back to make sure nobody was on his tail. He had heard the officer mention his name and wasn't about to stick around to find out all the details. He was sure Johansen would keep him informed. Crossing the parking lot, he jumped in his Maserati and rushed back home to collect his thoughts. He was upset that he couldn't see Deja, but he couldn't risk that officer finding out he was the match to the fingerprint on the shell casing.

Johansen had made a good point, but Paulie wasn't hearing it. He planned to pick up the drop at the warehouse, hit the streets hard getting the work off, and in between, hunt down and kill LB. Adamant about teaching LB a lesson, Paulie didn't care about nothing but taking the young nigga to class!

* * * * *

Down in South Philly, LB and Mikey were creeping through Country Cain's backyard. Country Cain was a fat nigga from Atlanta who relocated to Philly ten years ago. At first, niggas in the street weren't embracing the hustler from the south, but after he showed niggas around the way real love by having the lowest prices in the street on the white, the streets started treating and praising Country Cain like he was born and bred in their hood.

Country Cain felt more than comfortable in his Wharton Street apartment. He purchased a duplex, rented out the upstairs, and lived on the first floor. He knew the streets loved him.

LB and Mikey eased through the back alley with guns in hand. Reaching the back of the duplex, they made their way from window to window, peeping in. Dogs barked in the distance, while an occasional car drove past the end of the alley. It was three o'clock in the morning, and the house was pitch black.

"I think this is the nigga's room," Mikey said, standing on a cinderblock and looking in what he believed to be Country Cain's bedroom window.

LB rushed over and took position next to him on the block.

"Yeah, it got to be. Shit, you can hear the nigga snoring all the way out here," LB commented, then stepped off the block and walked around to the back door of the house.

"Whoa! Before you do that, hold up," Mikey said. He then went from window to window, carefully popping the screens off and trying to raise the windows up without making too much noise to wake Country Cain.

LB just stood back and watched. As soon as Mikey failed on his last window attempt, he reared back and slammed his size 12 foot into the door, knocking it off of its hinges. They didn't waste time, just in case someone in the house heard the entry. They moved through the house like police on a raid. By the time they got midway through the house, they heard Country Cain snoring; he was still knocked out.

"I'm going left. You go right," LB instructed before they

entered the bedroom where Country Cain laid in a deep sleep.

They stepped into the room, and with only a quick glance, they could see the man believed in luxury, even if he did live in an apartment. The room was beautifully furnished. They took position on both sides of the California king bed. LB took the liberty of waking the snoring man.

"Nigga, wake yo' fat ass up and break yo'self!" LB screamed.

To his surprise, the big man didn't move, but the person lying in bed with him did.

Trina, Kee's gold-digging friend, stuck her head from up under the covers still half asleep. As soon as she focused, her eyes got big as golf balls and her deafening scream pierced everyone's ears in the room. Country Cain stirred, then woke up and rolled over on his back.

"What the hell!" he spat groggily, looking from one man to the other as they kept their guns pointed at him and Trina.

Mikey took the honors of stepping over and slapping Trina with his free hand, a gesture to let them know they were serious.

"Bitch, scream like that again and I'm going to stick this gun in your mouth and pull the trigger," Mikey blurted as Trina held her face where he had slapped her.

Country Cain appeared to be calm, but what really had him nervous was the fact that both men were bare faced. He knew exactly what it meant when guns were pulled without masks.

"Say man, y'all got it! Just be easy with the gunplay. Shit, I'm from the streets just like y'all, and I totally respect the grind. All the money and dope is in the garage. Ain't no bucking on this end, player. Slippers count, and straight up, y'all caught my fat ass slippin'. Just keep it on the square, grab that stash, and be out," Country Cain said, trying to lighten the mood so the men wouldn't kill them.

"Nigga, I'm feeling that. So, you know what? I'm going to do just that. Real recognizes real. Enough said. Fam, what you think?" LB said, changing his mind about killing them.

"That you, LB? Tony's brother?" Trina called out, squinting in the dark room as she tried to see if it was the young hustler from her old hood.

It seemed like the whole room froze at Trina's recognition of LB. Country Cain's heart dropped. He knew with her recognizing the man that he would think twice about letting them live.

"Who you?" LB asked, walking over to get a closer look.

Country Cain tried his best to change the subject and rush the men out.

"Damn, Trina, let them do what they do. Y'all boys handle ya biz," Country Cain said, while giving Trina the evil eye.

"Man, this bitch knows you, bro. Twelve in the box, one on the stand," Mikey stated, referring to twelve jurors and one person on the witness stand. "Can't take that chance, bro." Mikey raised his gun while waiting on LB's reply.

"Yeah, I feel you...real talk," LB said, raising his gun, too.

"Wait! Hold up, y'all! Please, just get the money and bounce. Y'all ain't got to worry about no retaliation, no police, no nothing. My word, man. Ain't that right, Trina?" Country Cain yelled, then looked over at Trina.

Beyond mad that she had opened her mouth, Country Cain would have killed her himself if given a chance, especially if it would have saved his life.

"Yeah, y'all ain't got to worry about us, I swear," Trina pleaded, realizing her mistake.

"Man, fuck this!" Mikey screamed out.

LB looked at him and gave him the nod. Seconds later, shots

rang out.

Pop! Boom! Pop! Pop! Boom!

Country Cain tried his best to dodge the volley of shots coming his way. He even went as far as to grab Trina's small frame and try to use her as a shield.

"Aweee! Uhhh!" Trina screamed as she attempted to get out of the bed, but Country Cain's grip was too tight.

Both fell victim to the countless hollow points that came their way. Their bullet-riddled bodies laid intertwined like they were lovers cuddled up watching their favorite movie.

"Let's get this shit and go," LB called out as he turned and rushed out of the bedroom.

Mikey inspected the scene one more time before falling in step behind LB. It didn't take them long to find the stash in the one-car garage. After packing up the money and the bricks, they re-entered the house and exited out the same way they came in.

TONY STORY

CHAPTER 17

G STREET CHRONICLES
~A NEW URBAN DYNASTY~

WWW.GSTREETCHRONICLES.COM

The next day, Paulie was up with a lot on his mind.

"Boy, you locking shit down. Make sure you get at me when your other folks hit town. I'm going to give you some real fucking with if you jump that seven you say they want at one time," Paulie told Enod, one of his main customers.

"Sounds good. They will be hitting town late tonight, so I'll be at you tomorrow," he told Paulie, before getting behind the wheel of his Malibu and pulling off with the three blocks of cocaine he had just purchased.

Paulie was on his grind and at the same time packing his heat looking for LB. He knew he was going totally against the grain riding dirty, gunning for a nigga, but he didn't give a fuck. Paulie once played with the pistol as a hobby, robbing anybody holding. As soon as he was introduced to the dope game, he retired his gun except to use it for protection. After hearing Johansen tell him that Deja had been shot in his car, he strapped back up, and this time, it wasn't only for protection. He was on a manhunt for the young nigga responsible.

Riding down Diamond Street, he made a left in a known spot that he was told LB frequented. Baker Hill was a hangout for roughnecks from the Northside. They gathered to shoot dice, talk shit, and flex their ill-gotten gains. Paulie hit the block, cocked his .40 Glock, and lowered the speed of the Maserati to almost a stop. He crept along slowly, looking at the men standing around talking on cell phones, smoking weed, and selling drugs. A young nigga wearing a fitted hat, oversized bomber, and standing off in the distance on the side of the laundromat caught his attention. He pulled over next to the curb and jumped out the car.

"Say, my nigga," Paulie called out as he approached the boy, while brandishing the Glock.

The boy froze in his tracks.

"Yo, man, what's the beef?" The young boy held his hands in the air like he was surrendering.

"Where LB at? I know you know, so don't bullshit me, 'cause I'll kill your ass right here and now and think nothing of it." Paulie's tone was calm yet firm.

"LB came through here earlier with Mikey, man. That's all I can tell you 'cause I don't fuck with them niggas like that," the young boy replied nervously as he shook his hands in the air.

"Nigga, you fucking lying!" Paulie snapped, grabbing the young boy by his coat and jamming the gun against the side of his head, causing his hat to shift to the side.

"Man, I swear!" the young boy screamed, closing his eyes tight to brace for the blast.

Paulie released the boy's jacket and pushed him into an old grocery cart that sat on the side of the washhouse. The boy stumbled over it and fell to the ground.

Paulie didn't even bother tucking the gun as he stepped back off into the street. As soon as he was back in the car, two men rounded the building and walked over to the youngster who was getting up off of the ground.

"Yo, Lil' Spanky, what was all that about?" Chub asked with a hard scowl on his face.

"Nigga looking for LB," Spanky said, while dusting off his clothes and fixing his hat.

"Oh yeah? Nigga, I told you that nigga looked familiar. That was Ty's cousin Paulie! We should have wet that nigga's ass up, all in our hood looking for one of ours! Nigga, hit LB up and let him know that the nigga's out looking for him," Chub told Loon, who was looking up the block in the direction that Paulie had sped off in the Maserati.

"A'ight, damn! You said it, fuck!" Loon spat, then as he pulled out his cell phone to dial LB's number, he thought to himself, *Nigga, please come back down through here. I promise you won't be leaving out breathing.*

"Yeah?" LB answered coolly on the first ring, high off a fat blunt.

LB and Mikey were at Tony's old spot, which was now his spot. They sat around counting up last night's take and making calls to see who was in need of some good white. They had hit the block earlier to get some blunts and to put the word out about the cheap prices on the blow they held.

"Fam, that nigga Paulie just rode down through here waving a gun around looking for you. We really slipped on the bitch-ass nigga, but if he ride back through here, he won't make it out, real talk," Loon said, while Chub watched a couple of young hustlers run to a car trying to make a drug sale.

"Man, fuck that bitch-made ass nigga. I got this four-pound

locked and cocked, ready to introduce the nigga. He better hope he catch me before I catch him, because it's going to be a closed casket for his ass," LB said with a slight slur, feeling high and floating.

"We need to ride hard on that nigga, fam, non-stop 'til we body his fuck ass!" Mikey spoke with venom in his tone as he pulled on the blunt and played with the smoke.

"Tell that boy Mikey I said what up. But really, my nigga, that nigga Paulie really done disrespected the game riding down through here looking for one of ours. You know we got to punish the nigga for his bravery. We out here bumping now, so if the nigga decide to ride back through, we'll be on his ass. Y'all boys hit me and let me know what it do."

Loon rushed to cut the call short as he watched Lady and Fransisca, two hood divas, pull up in a red Mustang.

"A'ight, my nigga," LB muttered, then clicked off the line and sat up on the couch. "This nigga is really tripping, looking for me in my own hood," he spat, like the news had just sunk in.

"Bro, that nigga know it's on!" Mikey added, then pulled an AK-47 from the side of the couch and started to load it.

* * * * *

Paulie slapped the steering wheel, hating that he couldn't find LB to finish him off. Just as he was about to hit the main road, he slammed on the brakes and turned the car around. He would circle the block one more time to see if he could catch that nigga slipping.

TONY STORY

CHAPTER 18

G STREET CHRONICLES
~A NEW URBAN DYNASTY~

WWW.GSTREETCHRONICLES.COM

"Johansen, I'm glad you could make it! I'm excited about breaking this case. Ain't I something? I almost got this whole case wrapped up with a bow, when those tight-wad asses in them suits who were chosen over me couldn't find their own ass with a flashlight," Carter bellowed, as he stepped to the side so Johansen could enter his modest three-bedroom row house off of City Line Avenue.

"Yeah, Carter, you've done a great job unraveling this whole thing, because really, I was dumbfounded with the little we had to go on. I guess I'm one of those guys with the flashlight who can't find my ass, huh?" Johansen laughed and slapped his old friend on the back as he entered the house.

"Come on now, buddy. You know you are nothing like those tight asses in them tight suits. Shit, I learned watching you!" Carter said jokingly.

The two men made their way to the back of the house where Carter had converted his dining room into a home office. Johansen looked around the room in amazement. Carter had his office completely set up, with white dry eraser boards and all. He could run a full-fledge operation from his home. It was obvious the man lived alone.

"I hear you, old buddy. A'ight, what are we working with here? Do we have enough to report to the higher-ups to get a warrant for this Paulie guy?" Johansen asked, eyeing all the files, notes, and bagged-up evidence Carter had unlawfully removed from the crime scene. Johansen even noticed that Carter had pulled evidence from the evidence room and brought it home.

"Boy, I got this puzzle all pieced together. However, there was something else I found that was very odd about this whole investigation, but before I started pointing fingers, I wanted to make sure my assumptions were correct." Carter pulled his glasses out of his pocket and put them on.

"Assumptions? What you got brewing, Carter?" Johansen asked, taking a seat at the table and looking over all the evidence laid out before them.

"Partner, you are not going to believe this. I think we got someone trying to cover up for this guy, or there are some very incompetent agents in the department. I'm going with the first one." Carter grabbed a file folder off the table and flipped it open.

Johansen already knew the mistakes he had made while trying to cover up for Paulie. As Carter flipped through the file, Johansen discreetly eased his small caliber backup pistol from his side. By the time Carter found what he was looking for, Johansen was standing up with the gun pointed to the back of his head.

"Budd—"

Pop! Pop!

Johansen squeezed the trigger twice, cutting off Carter's last words. Carter's head jerked forward twice. Then he slumped face first onto the cherry oak wooden table next to his computer desk. Johansen quickly grabbed up everything and stuffed it back in the bag that sat on the table. After making sure everything was clean at the scene, Johansen exited the residence with the bag and a murder on his hands. Just as he approached the expressway entrance, his phone rang.

"Hello?"

"The drop is there. Just make sure your boy gets back on his shit, 'cause we need this stuff moved before the end of the week," Wink, one of Miami's biggest Cartel bosses, said as he lounged around in the sunroom of his five-million-dollar home.

"I got it all covered," Johansen replied, heading east to look for a good spot to dispose of the evidence.

G STREET CHRONICLES
~A NEW URBAN DYNASTY~

WWW.GSTREETCHRONICLES.COM

TONY STORY

CHAPTER 19

TONY STORY

G STREET CHRONICLES
A NEW URBAN DYNASTY

WWW.GSTREETCHRONICLES.COM

As soon as Paulie turned around and started making his way back through the hood for a second time to look for LB, his cell phone rang.

"What up?" he answered in an irritated tone.

He had been trying to contact Johansen ever since rushing out of the hospital yesterday, and now he was ringing his phone when he's on the hunt for this young nigga. Bad timing indeed.

"Couldn't get back with you last night, but listen, your ass is covered and the shipment is there. Grab what you need and handle it, 'cause I got something to deal with right quick. I'll meet you back out at the warehouse later. I hope you heard what I was telling you yesterday. It's time to get back to business," Johansen said, getting fed up with having to hold Paulie's hand and hoping he did the right thing.

After an arrest and interrogation, Johansen had chosen Paulie to work with seeing that he was a standup guy. Not only was he a loyal, solid dude, he also had a clientele that bought product on the regular. The shipments were getting bigger and the buying wasn't slowing down at all. Johansen knew Paulie was a real go-getter, and that's why he had to keep him safe. He was a very valuable piece of his plans to get rich, retire, and get him a black, big booty mistress.

"Yeah, I'm back to business. I'm heading out there now. What was the dude at the hospital talking about?" Paulie inquired as he turned and headed out of the hood toward the expressway.

"You and some evidence that could link you to a murder scene. Don't worry about it; you're all good. Just handle that biz," Johansen assured him.

He exited onto the drive in the 23rd and Ridge area and looked for a good spot to dispose of the evidence. Just as Johansen hit the back alley, he saw two bums standing around a big barrel with a roaring fire blazing out of it. They were rubbing their hands together trying to stay warm.

"Damn…a'ight," Paulie said, ending the call. He was glad Johansen was on his team.

Johansen pulled his unmarked car up next to the men. When they looked at him and realized he was the law, they sprinted off. He didn't even look in the men's direction. He just dumped the evidence into the barrel of fire and watched it burn.

* * * * *

Thirty minutes later, Paulie pulled up to the warehouse. As he looked around the parking lot, he had a gut feeling something wasn't right. He pulled around to the back and looked around. He peeped a man on the roof who looked as if he was trying his best to stay out of view. Another man walked through the back parking lot of the warehouse with a newspaper cuffed under his arm, while drinking a cup of coffee and looking around suspiciously.

Paulie looked over at unit 411, the place where the shipment sat waiting for distribution. He put the car in park, then changed his mind. Feeling something just wasn't right, he shifted the car in drive and pulled back out the lot. He decided to ride over to New Jersey to The Cherry Hill Mall until he could talk to Johansen.

TONY STORY

CHAPTER 20

G STREET CHRONICLES
~A NEW URBAN DYNASTY~

WWW.GSTREETCHRONICLES.COM

Days had gone by, and Stu was still stressing over his partner's death. It really bothered him that this nigga took his partner's life after he stood strong for him and did five years. He jumped in his old pickup and rode through Philly with a pistol-grip pump, looking to finish the job Paulie had paid him and Killa to do. He rode down 15th Street, heading toward South Philly to the hood where he used to hang out, which was the same hood he had first met Tony and his wild little brother, LB. As Stu cruised to the spot, he thought about that day...

"Say, money, we good on that, right?" Tony asked Stu, who sat thinking about the proposition just offered to him.

"Run that by me again. Slower this time," Stu said, turning to face Tony as they stood in front of Lucky's corner store.

Just as Tony started to speak, LB cut him off.

"This nigga? Be for real. He don't even look like a killer," LB stated as he walked over and stood with the men.

Stu looked over at Tony, then at LB and frowned.

"Lil' nigga, chill. Bruh certified. He going to handle the nigga. Like I

was saying, when you run up in the nigga's spot and get the play, just break me off half and you get the rest," Tony said, playing on Stu's intelligence.

Tony knew Cash, the well-known pill man from 7th Street, was holding a lot of cash and pills in his spot. LB had already done some investigating on the lick, but Tony called him off of it because Cash wasn't a lightweight and stayed strapped.

After pulling LB off the lick, Tony got in touch with Stu, the crazy killer from around the way. Stu was crazy, but giving Tony half the goods on the lick would make him both crazy and stupid.

After hearing Tony out, he looked up in the air at the darkening clouds and smiled. When he looked back at the two men, he changed his smile into a frown and emphasized his true feelings using the chrome .9mm he held to Tony's head.

LB's mouth dropped wide open, but nothing came out. He was in shock.

"Look, nigga, don't ever play Stu for a fool. Now, this is how it's going to go. I'm going to go up in that nigga's shit and body him. After that, I'm going to take everything he got and split it three ways…me, myself, and you. That sounds better, right?" Stu spat as he opened and closed his hand, getting a better grip on the butt of the gun.

"My nigga, you dead right. I like that split," Tony agreed, trying his best not to anger the crazed killer.

"That's what's up, man," Stu said, lowering the gun and tucking it back in his waist.

LB took a step back, about to blast Stu for disrespecting his brother. Tony recognized the look in his younger brother's eyes. He made eye contact with LB, and LB immediately recognized the look. Tony was shook at first, then his nervousness turned to anger. But, then, he calmed down because he knew Stu was mentally unstable, and he needed him for the lick…

Stu was sure he would be able to find young LB somewhere around the block.

As the sun set, hustlers were out in full blast, serving every junkie that walked the street looking for a fix. LB sat on the hood of a broken down station wagon parked a block over from his place. He was waiting on Mikey to get back from his baby mama Ella's crib so they could resume their mission of finding Paulie. He was determined to find Paulie and off him before Paulie caught him slipping. Even though he knew niggas were gunning for him, he still kept a cool head. He felt safe on his block, especially since he had his new friend, Betsy, with him. Betsy was his .40 Glock with an extended clip.

LB popped a pill, took a heavy sip of the Lean, and pulled on the blunt all in one motion. After hitting the blunt a second time, he looked from left to right, then from front to back, checking out his surroundings. He kept his composure because he didn't fear man or death.

Stu crossed Belk Street and entered into LB's stomping grounds. He rode by the laundromat, a known hangout spot for young hustlers looking for some fat sacks of weed and a good game of dice. Turning on the block, Stu noticed a young nigga wearing a bright red do-rag waving him down.

"Hey, yo! Yo!" the young hustler called out, thinking Stu was a junkie looking for a hit.

Stu hit the brakes on the truck, stopping in the middle of the street. Out of nowhere, three other young niggas, including the one who flagged him down, raced toward the truck. Stu reached over, picked up the pump off the seat, and looked through his rearview at them approaching. The first young hustler almost had a heart attack when he leaned in the truck trying to make a sale and looked directly into the barrel of the eight-shot pistol-grip pump.

"Oh shit! My bad, homie!" The boy jumped back, almost falling over the curb.

Not paying attention, the other young hustlers got the same thing—the pistol-grip in their faces.

"Fuck!" the other young hustlers yelled as they turned and hurried away from the pick-up truck.

Stu hoped one of the lil' niggas would be LB so he wouldn't have to ride around looking for him, but none were him. So, he lifted his foot off the brake and brought his right foot down on the gas, still on the hunt.

* * * * *

"Man, something wasn't right out at the warehouse. We need to check into that," Paulie told Johansen, who was entering his home after disposing of the evidence he had gotten from Carter.

"What you mean something wasn't right? Look, Paulie, I don't have time for this paranoid bullshit! We need that shipment hitting the streets today! My people made sure everything was in check on the delivery, and now it's on me...us...to get rid of this shit. I'll be out at the warehouse around nine o'clock tonight. Meet me there," Johansen ordered, as his wife of twenty years entered the front room where he stood holding the phone.

"I hear you, man, but I'm telling you, something ain't right. How about you make a couple calls around and see if anything is going on out there?" Paulie suggested, while turning into the mall parking lot.

"Yeah, okay. I'll do that. You just be there at nine o'clock, 'cause we need to get this stuff in the streets where it belongs." Johansen said, as his wife Caroline looked at him with a frown on her face.

"A'ight, I'll be there." Paulie disconnected the call and found a parking space in the busy lot.

Caroline's face turned beet red and her right eye started to twitch from anger.

"You're still messing around with that stuff, Claude? You promised me that you were going to leave all of that crooked business alone and live right! For God's sake, how would it look for us, a police detective and a retired district attorney, to be involved in such crazy dealings?" she screamed at him, while standing directly in front of him with her arms folded across her chest.

Johansen took a deep breath, leaned over, and hugged her.

"Honeybun, this is the last of it, I promise. I'm sorry, sweetie. My word…this is it," he again promised her, then planted a kiss on her forehead.

* * * * *

Stu turned right at one corner and then made another right at the next, determined to find LB. He was only a block over from where LB was kicked back enjoying the evening breeze, smoking on a blunt, and waiting on Mikey. Stu cruised down the block slowly, looking from left to right, hoping to scope out his target. Pulling up at the next stop sign, Stu contemplated between a left and a right turn, then made a left, which was LB's block. Clearing the white delivery truck parked close to the corner, he smiled as he eyed his target. He hit the gas on the truck, sending it speeding forward. Just as he got a few feet from his target, he slammed on the brakes and jumped out. The young hustler struck out after seeing the man with the pistol running toward him. Stu smiled a sinister smile as he leveled the gun and pulled the trigger.

Boom!

The young hustler was lucky he tripped over the curb as the slug whistled by him, missing him by inches.

"Ahh!" the boy yelled, falling face first on the concrete and dropping his small baggies filled with diced-up pieces of crack.

Stu was on him, ready to take another shot. He stood over the man like the Grim Reaper ready to consume a soul. When the boy turned over and looked up at Stu, he lost control of his bladder. Stu put the pistol in the boy's face, and that's when he realized he had the wrong person. The boy wasn't LB.

"Fuck!" Stu screamed, as the young boy looked up at him with pleading eyes.

"Ma...ma...mannn! Please, man!" the young boy pleaded, not knowing why the man was about to kill him.

"Fuck-ass bullshit!" Stu growled. Beyond pissed, he wanted to pull the trigger anyway. Instead, he lowered the gun, turned, and just walked away.

The young boy couldn't move. He just lay there trying to catch his breath. The stench of the piss that soaked the front of his pants wavered through the air and up to his nose. He leaned up on one elbow and watched as Stu walked off.

Just as Stu turned away from the hustler, he looked right into the eyes of the man who he had been looking for. He and LB locked eyes.

TONY STORY

CHAPTER 21

G STREET CHRONICLES
~A NEW URBAN DYNASTY~

WWW.GSTREETCHRONICLES.COM

Paulie decided to make a couple rounds through the mall to clear his mind. He hadn't been in there a good five minutes before he heard his name being called.

"Hey, Paulie! Paulie!"

He looked to see who was calling him and saw Cynt, one of Philly's most known boosters, heading in his direction with a bag that he knew contained some expensive gear. Paulie had stopped shopping with Cynt over a year ago when his money could afford him a more expensive taste of clothes, threads that were beyond what she could steal for him. The places where he shopped had security that was way too advanced even for one of the slickest boosters in the city.

"What up, lady?" Paulie called out as he waited for her to catch up with him.

"Hey, boy! You still looking good! You and I know you would look a lot better in some of these." Cynt reached in her bag and separated the clothes so he could see a pair of olive green designer jeans.

"Now you know I ain't rocking none of that no more," Paulie told her, but Cynt wasn't one to give up on a sale.

Cynt made a lot of money in the city. She used her good looks and persuasive words to her advantage. Cynt wasn't the average booster. She was a dime piece by all standards and a soft-spoken, slick talker.

"Paulie, baby, the women going crazy about these! How you ain't rocking 'em?" Cynt cooed, now holding the jeans up next to Paulie, trying to enforce her sale.

"Baby girl, I'm good. You ready to be mine yet?" Paulie asked. He had been trying to get the lesbian between his sheets ever since he met her.

"Oh no, you didn't! You know my bitch ain't going for that. I'm married anyway," Cynt said, smiling while holding up her hand and showing him the ring her lesbian lover had given her.

"Oh, you ain't switch back yet? Damn. Seriously, though, I'm good. Just keep me in mind when you convert," Paulie said jokingly, then walked off.

"Oh, Paulie!"

Paulie stopped and turned to face Cynt. "What up?"

"What I first called you for is to tell you folks talking about Tony's people are looking for you. They also talking about Kee was killed 'cause she helped you set Tony up. Paulie, shit is crazy out here. Not to mention, they found Trina, Kee's best friend, and that boy from Atlanta who they call Country Cain, dead… all shot up. The streets are really going crazy," Cynt said, folding the jeans and putting them back in the bag.

"Yeah, shit is definitely getting crazy. It's my first time hearing about Trina. That's fucked up," Paulie stated, shaking his head, hating to hear that his boy Curt's baby mama had been killed.

"Yeah, I'm getting out of Philly as soon as my boo finishes her hours in cosmetology school. Goodbye to Philly and hey to Atlanta! Paulie, be careful. I'll be seeing you around." Cynt grabbed her bags, turned around, and walked away.

Paulie ran his hand over the .9mm Ruger tucked in his waist as he made his way through the busy mall.

* * * * *

"Are you going to be back home in time for dinner?" Caroline asked Johansen, as he grabbed his keys off the kitchen counter and put his jacket on.

"Yes, dear. I'm just going to get this business over with," he replied, then exited the house and climbed behind the wheel of his Crown Vic.

Before pulling out of the driveway, he flipped open his cell phone and called Paulie.

"Paulie, I'm heading to the warehouse a little early, so just meet me out there any time before nine o'clock," Johansen told him as he put the car in drive and pulled off.

"Did you call and check to see if anything was going down out there?" Paulie asked, while browsing the new leathers Nordstrom's had just gotten in.

"Yeah, I made the calls, and like I told you, everything is good. You got to stop being so paranoid," Johansen lied as he merged into the evening traffic.

"Guess I'm just too much on point, but that's all good. I'll be right out there after I leave the mall," Paulie said, now checking out the designer loafers.

"I'll have everything ready for you when you get there."

Johansen ended the call and turned up the Willie Nelson playing on his cheap stereo system.

Johansen knew this drop was going to be the one to put him on top. After moving the product, he would finally be in a comfortable position that his measly state salary couldn't afford. He planned to tell his supplier, Wink, that things on his end were not safe anymore and that he had to gracefully bow out, but he would hook him up with Paulie to keep things moving for him.

Everything was falling right in place for Johansen, and he wasn't about to let anything or anyone mess it up, even if it meant ending one's existence. It was his last year before retirement, his bank account was nearing the seven-figure mark, and his car and house were paid off. The only thing he lacked was his black exotic mistress. This last run would have him sitting like a king.

He merged into the right lane and activated his turn signal. As far as he could see, there was nothing peculiar about the warehouse parking lot. He turned into the parking lot, pulled up in front of unit 411, and killed the car's engine. He secured his .38 special in his shoulder holster and got out. Before approaching the door, he looked around, trying to see if he picked up the same vibe Paulie had. Seeing everything was clear, he dismissed the paranoid thoughts and replaced them with big-money luxury fantasies.

The DEA and FBI agents stayed in position and out of sight, waiting for someone to enter the warehouse and claim the drug shipment that belonged to a man who went by the name of Wink. They hoped he would be the one to show, but knew that was highly unlikely since he rarely left the comforts of his Beverly Hills mansion. They banked on trying to bust in with other evidence and bring Wink down, putting him out of business for good.

"Hey, get him up out of there. He's about to blow our cover," one of the agents on the scene told his subordinate over the radio as they watched Johansen exit the official car.

Just as the subordinate was about to make a dash from behind the building, he was halted by the next order.

"All units hold your position. I repeat, all units hold your position," the commanding agent called out, watching as Johansen pulled the keys to the warehouse unit from his pocket and approached the door.

"He's got the keys to this place? Ain't he—" the agent started, but was cut off by the agent behind him.

"Yeah, he's one of us. I hate fucking crooked cops. I can't wait to bust his ass wide open," the second agent spat. He anxiously awaited the call to move in.

"Everybody stand by. We'll converge when he's inside," the commander barked into the radio.

All the agents waited patiently for Johansen to open the door and enter the warehouse unit. Using his key to unlock the door, he pushed it open and stepped in. Closing the door behind him, he walked over to the shipment and started inspecting the boxes. By the time he had a couple of boxes open checking out the contents, the warehouse door crashed in.

"What the hell?" Johansen turned and set his eyes on the FBI and DEA units who were rushing through the door.

He knew it was no use trying to run, but he did it anyway.

"Freeze!" the DEA front man screamed.

Johansen thought about his wife's words as he took off running through the warehouse. He silently prayed to God that if he got away, he would leave it all alone. The money and lavish life he'd done it all for didn't look so appealing anymore. He ran as hard and fast as his fifty-six-year-old legs could take him, but he didn't get far.

"Stop right there!" the FBI agent screamed, leveling his pistol at an out-of-breath Johansen, who had run himself into a corner.

Johansen knew if he went to jail at his age, it would be equivalent to a life sentence. Therefore, he did what he thought was best.

"He's pulling a weapon!" the head agent shouted, prompting the other agents to open fire.

Pop! Pop! Bang! Boom! Pop!

The bullets from the high-powered automatic weapons tore through Johansen with ease. The first chest shot penetrated his heart, killing him instantly. The following shots were only practice for the agents. The shooting ceased when he fell into a stack of pallets, spread eagle with his gun in his clutch.

* * * * *

When Paulie pulled up on the main road outside of the warehouse, he saw police and emergency vehicles everywhere. He knew his feelings from earlier had to have been on point. He picked up his phone and dialed Johansen's number. Getting the voicemail on both attempts, he pulled the car into the neighboring business' parking lot and got out. He blended in with the other warehouse workers and watched the FBI and DEA carry boxes of drugs from the unit.

"What happened over there?" Paulie asked the young, perky white girl who was flicking pictures with her cell phone.

"It was wild, dude! They busted that warehouse. It was fuckin' full of drugs, man. Somebody got put on ice, though. Brought 'em out on the stretcher and tossed 'em in the meat wagon. Shit was like..."

She went on and on excitedly, as Paulie turned and walked back to his car.

* * * * *

"Noooo!" Mrs. Johansen screamed when the agents arrived at her home to deliver the news of her husband's death, while also serving her with a search warrant and confiscation papers.

The FBI seized all the property listed in Johansen's name, which was everything. They also advised Mrs. Johansen on whom to contact about their joint bank account that had been frozen, as well.

"Sorry, ma'am, but when you deal with people who are involved in stuff like this, this is what happens," the young gung-ho agent told her, while the other agents descended on the house.

"Yes, yes, I understand," Caroline mumbled.

She waited until everyone was consumed with their searching, before quietly walking away and slipping into her bedroom.

"Where is she?" the agent asked, looking over at the recliner where she had just been sitting.

"I don't know. Shit, she's a retired DA. You know she ain't going too far. I'll get her and put her in—"

Pop!

The single gunshot cut the agent off mid-sentence. All of the agents stopped in their tracks, pulled their weapons, and ducked for cover. After a few minutes, they rushed upstairs from where the sound of the shot came.

"Mrs. Johansen, come on out!" the agent shouted, while flanking her bedroom door.

Not hearing a response from Mrs. Johansen, the first agent eased up and kicked in the thin wooden bedroom door. Mrs. Johansen was laid across the bed with a picture of her and her husband taken on their last vacation next to her, a pistol in her hand, and a gunshot wound to her head.

"Call medics!" the agent barked into his radio.

"No need. She's dead, and whoever didn't secure her when we entered is up shit's creek," the veteran agent said firmly, while looking over at Mrs. Johansen, whose head laid open like a ripe watermelon.

"Damn!" the rookie mumbled, knowing he was responsible.

TONY STORY

CHAPTER 22

G STREET CHRONICLES
~A NEW URBAN DYNASTY~

WWW.GSTREETCHRONICLES.COM

LB looked into Stu's eyes and saw death. Stu recognized LB on sight. LB hesitated for a moment, and then it hit him that Stu was the one paid to off him. LB dropped his blunt and cup as Stu raised his pistol and pulled the trigger.

Boom! Boom!

The shotgun blast echoed through the air, bringing the block's residents to their windows. LB rolled off of the old car and scurried away like a rat running for its life. Stu didn't let up one bit, though. He took off behind LB blasting shots, determined to finish the job. LB bent the first corner, running full speed trying to get away. The Lean and Kush had him slightly off balance, but he managed to stay steady as he ran through the alley behind the row houses. As soon as he got a safe distance away from Stu, he reached in his waist for his .45 automatic, but realized it wasn't there.

"Fuck! Shit!" he cursed, looking back in the direction he had just run from, knowing he had dropped it while fleeing.

Stu stopped mid-stride when LB disappeared in the brush. He turned and headed back to his truck.

"Fuck nigga, it's on now! Nigga, it's war!" LB screamed as he cut through the alleyway to his crew's hanging spot.

Mikey parked the Delta '88 and got out, about to head up to LB's place. Just as he stepped up on the curb, he saw Stu coming from his right with his pistol in plain view. Mikey recognized the known killer instantly.

"Stu, what it do, my nigga? Boy, I see you ain't playin'," Mikey said, unaware that Stu had been busting shots at his right-hand man just a short while ago.

"Can't play with these bitches. You good?" Stu asked the young nigga, whose uncle used to run with Stu back in the day.

"I'm good, OG. Be easy," Mikey said, as he looked up at the man with known mental health issues holding the pump.

"Yeah," Stu said before calmly walking back to his truck. Still on the hunt for his prey, he put the gear shift in the drive and hit the next block.

Mikey walked up and knocked on LB's door, but didn't get an answer.

After knocking a few more times, Lil' Bobby, the youngster from across the street, ran up on him.

"What up, lil' nigga? Where LB at?" Mikey asked Bobby, while looking around.

"That nigga you was just talking to chased him up the street with that big gun. LB ran like a bitch!" Bobby laughed, covering his mouth with both hands.

"What?" Mikey asked, making sure he had heard Lil' Bobby right.

"The man that you was talking to chased him up the block

with that gun. LB scary!"

Lil' Bobby laughed again as he turned and hopped down the three steps one at a time, then took off running around the corner.

* * * * *

"Boy, what you got going on? Slow down, playa," Loon said as LB ran down the back alley where his crew was smoking weed and telling war stories.

The whole crew stood up when LB ran up in the spot.

"That fuckin' Stu nigga's blasting! Who holding?" LB asked, breathing hard. He knew every man in the circle was packing heat.

"Here, nigga, take this." Loon handed him a .380.

LB grabbed the small handgun and held it up with two fingers.

"Nigga, what the fuck am I going to do with this? Give me that shit!" LB called out to Snowman, who had his .45 tucked in his waist.

"Fuck you then, killa!" Loon said playfully, snatching back his .380.

"This is what I'm talking about right here," LB stated when Snowman passed him the piece. He held it up and cocked it.

"Let's roll, y'all. We going to handle this bitch nigga," Loon said as the crew fell in behind him and LB.

They covered the blocks quickly, looking to catch up with the shooter. A few minutes later, they were on LB's block looking for Stu. As soon as they bent the corner, they saw Mikey being handcuffed and put into the back of a police car. The officer searching Mickey's Delta '88 held up a handgun and a bag of Kush for his fellow officer to see.

"Po Po...hold up!" LB told his crew, waving them over to the side.

They watched the police load Mikey into the patrol car and drive off.

TONYSTORY

CHAPTER 23

G STREET CHRONICLES
A NEW URBAN DYNASTY

WWW.GSTREETCHRONICLES.COM

Paulie headed up Lombard Street toward the expressway. He was going to check on Deja, who had just been released from the hospital. He knew the remaining work he had at the house was his last, so he picked up the phone and called Rubio, his Mexican connect.

"Who speak?" Rubio asked, sitting in the back office of his car customization shop that was located on the north side of Atlanta.

"This is Paulie, old friend. How's it going?" Paulie asked as he merged into midday traffic.

"Hey, Paulie, my friend. Where you been?" Rubio hadn't heard from Paulie since Johansen had been keeping a steady flow of some of the best cocaine to hit the city of Philly.

"I've been working, but the company I've been contracting with isn't getting jobs like they used to. So, I'm networking for more jobs," Paulie said, knowing Rubio would read between the lines.

"Oh yeah? Well, my friend, I have someone who may be able

to help you. How about you meet us for dinner soon," Rubio replied, letting him know he'd rather talk face to face.

"Okay, sounds good. How about Saturday?" Paulie figured that would give him more than enough time to tie up loose ends in the city before he flew out to Atlanta.

"That works. I'll see you Saturday."

Paulie disconnected the call as he approached his exit.

* * * * *

Saturday rolled around in no time. He had hit the streets hard one more time searching for LB, but with no success. He dumped the remainder of work he had on hand and stashed over a quarter mill for re-up. He looked at his watch as he exited his spot and climbed in his Maserati, heading for the airport. His flight departed at 12:34 p.m., so he would be in Atlanta no later than 2:25 p.m. After arriving at the airport, he parked his ride in the Park & Ride lot and caught the shuttle to the terminal. He got there just in time.

"Flight 112 to Atlanta now boarding," the attendant announced over the airport's PA system when Paulie was a few feet away from his departure gate.

Paulie noticed several ladies checking him out. Dressed in a soft, light blue leather jacket, sparkling jewelry, and dark designer frames, he stood out in the small crowd. He looked like a celebrity without the entourage.

"Headed home or just visiting?" the petite, scantily dressed woman adorned in Chanel gear from head to toe asked Paulie as she boarded the plane behind him.

"Just visiting. What about you?" he asked, already knowing

the answer from her southern drawl when she spoke.

"Headed back home to the city. My girl from Philly got me up here, talking about how much money I could make in the clubs up north. Please, I can't tell. Shit was whack as hell. Y'all don't even make it rain up here," the woman complained as they looked for their seats, which just happened to be across from each other.

Paulie laughed and shook his head. The petite girl was absolutely gorgeous. Her C-cup breasts, wide hips, and plump ass fit her perfectly. Paulie checked her out from head to toe and couldn't find a mark, blemish, or hair out of place.

"I feel you, 'cause ain't nothing like the down south strip clubs. They crazy off the chain. By the way, my name is Paulie," he said, extending his hand to her across the aisle.

"I'm Sashay," she replied, admiring the sparkling diamond ring on his middle finger.

"Good to meet you, beautiful," Paulie added, licking his lips.

His words and gestures caught Sashay totally off guard.

"Umph...it's good to meet you, too. How long are you going to be in Atlanta?" she asked, as her gaze landed on the iced-out diamond chain that was visible at the top of his black t-shirt.

"For a few days. How about you be my tour guide?" Paulie suggested playfully.

"How about I just be your company until you leave? Tour guides ain't built like this," Sashay gave herself a once over and then looked back up seductively at Paulie.

"Ooookay" Paulie slowly replied as the plane took off en route to the ATL.

* * * * *

"Man, you sure this is where that nigga lay his head?" Loon asked LB.

The two were creeping through the backyard of the house that was next to Stu's crib.

"Man, Mikey's uncle use to run with this fool, and everybody knows where this nigga lay his head. They just too shook to come see 'bout this fool," LB told him as they rounded the house to the street. "That's the nigga's truck."

"We need to get this nigga to the door," Loon said, looking around.

"I got a way. Follow me." LB led Loon to Stu's neighbor's house.

Knock! Knock! Knock!

"Yes?" a Haitian lady who had to be well into her eighties called out.

"Excuse me, ma'am, could you help us? We about to surprise our uncle who hasn't seen us in years. He lives next door to you. Could you do us a favor and knock on his door for us?" LB asked with fake excitement in his tone.

Opening the door, the old lady frowned while looking from LB to Loon.

"I ain't 'bout to go near that crazy fool's house! He ain't right; he the devil himself!" the lady snapped, then slammed the door in their faces.

"So much for that. Hold up! There the nigga go right there," Loon said.

They both paused and watched Stu step out on his front porch with his pit bull.

"Let's do this, nigga," LB said.

Both men pulled out their heat and crossed Stu's neighbor's yard, heading in his direction.

By the time Stu looked up, it was too late. Loon and LB had their guns raised and were blasting. Stu tried to run back inside the house, but the spray of bullets stopped him cold. They let loose shot after shot while running up on him. The pit bull even took a shot to the head and keeled over with a loud yelp. Stu's body shook as each shot penetrated his back. He held the doorknob in a tight, bloody grip as he fell facedown into his house.

"Yeah, bitch nigga, you fucked with the wrong one this time!" LB jumped on the porch and delivered two shots to the back of Stu's head.

"We out! Let's go, my nigga!" Loon yelled.

They broke out running around the back of the house to their getaway car that was parked a block over.

The little old Haitian lady looked out her window and over at Stu who was laying lifeless in the doorway. She just shook her head and went back to watering her plants, not bothering to call the police.

* * * * *

By the time the plane landed, Paulie and Sashay knew each other well. Paulie offered her a ride in his rental, but she had her car already at the airport.

"What's a good time to call?" she asked Paulie as they exited the terminal.

"Hit me 'bout nine o'clock tonight. My business should be finished by then." Paulie took in her curves, anticipating her nakedness later.

"Okay, I'll do that. You said you staying at the W, right?" Sashay asked, looking him up and down.

"Yeah," Paulie answered.

As she turned and walked off, throwing her hips and ass from side to side, he couldn't help but to stare.

* * * * *

After checking into his room at the W, Paulie took a quick shower and changed before leaving to meet with Rubio. This was his third invite to Rubio's hometown, but he had never actually sat at his dinner table. Rubio would always meet him at Ruth's Chris, where they would discuss business. Once he showered and got dressed, he called to confirm their meeting.

"Hey, friend, you in town?" Rubio was going over numbers as he sat at his desk in his shop.

"Yeah. Same place, right?" Paulie asked, already knowing the drill.

"You know I'm a creature of habit. Same place, six o'clock. Is that good for you?" He already knew Paulie would agree.

"Yeah, that's fine. I'll be there," Paulie replied as he looked out over the beautiful Atlanta skyline.

"Good...good. See you then." Rubio ended the call.

Paulie took out the time to call Deja to check on her. It was obvious she was okay based on the fact she was up and moving around. After talking with her, he sat around flipping the TV until it was time for him to meet with Rubio. Looking at his Movado, he saw it was 5:30 p.m.

He left his jacket in the room since the Atlanta weather didn't call for it and headed downstairs to the Dodge Charger he had rented. Easily remembering the directions from his two previous visits, he pulled out the parking lot, and arrived at Ruth's Chris ten minutes later. He asked the waiter for a corner table so they could be out of earshot of the other patrons. He pulled out his phone, clicked on the Philadelphia news app, and read the news while waiting on Rubio to arrive.

The new Cadillac Fleetwood pulled slowly into the lot and parked. The pearl jumping out of the high-gloss gold paint could be seen a mile away. The chrome 22's sparkled under the evening sun. Rubio had a fleet of some of the most sleek, customized vehicles in the city. The Fleetwood he rode in that day was his pride and joy. He had personally customized the vehicle from the ground up. He had taken the new car, dismantled it, and then built it back up. It was now fit for a car show.

He decided to park to the far side of the lot so it wouldn't be scratched or dented by careless drivers. Rubio then stepped out the car and placed his titanium frames over his beady grey eyes. One would think for him to hold so much weight within the Mexican Cartel, he would be a much bigger man. But, Rubio was only 5'4" and weighed 150 pounds. He also looked much younger than his forty-one years of age. One fact about Rubio that rang true was that he didn't have a Napoleon complex. Knowing his power and position within, he carried himself like a giant, never factoring in his size.

Paulie saw as the little man entered the restaurant dressed in a pair of dingy jeans, fitted t-shirt, and an expensive gold chain.

"Hey!" Paulie called out from the far corner, while waving his hand in the air for Rubio to see.

Hearing Paulie, Rubio looked over and waved, acknowledging

his presence as he headed in his direction.

"Hey, Paulie, it's good to see you again," Rubio said.

Paulie stood and gave him a firm handshake.

"Same here, friend," Paulie replied, releasing his grip.

They both took a seat and got right down to business.

"So what's the deal? What are you looking to purchase, and do you wish for me to handle shipping or you already got that covered?" Rubio asked, removing his frames from his face and laying them on the table in front of him.

Paulie paused and thought before answering, because he knew the price would go up at least fifty percent if Rubio had to ship it. Then he thought of a way to get it back up top to Philly himself. After thinking things over thoroughly, he answered.

"I'm going to need you to handle the shipping. I will make any necessary arrangements that need to be made when I get back home," Paulie said, leaning back in his chair.

"I will ship. You don't have to do anything but pick up your product when it's time. I will handle all arrangements," Rubio told him, already knowing he would use his car collision shop in Jersey to handle the delivery.

"Okay, sounds good. So, um…what we talking? How much a brick?" Paulie asked and then braced himself for the price, knowing it would be nothing close to Johansen's tag.

"For you, with delivery, I give 'em to you for twenty-six a brick. I got some of the purest shit you'll ever touch. You can step on this shit two or three times, and it'll still knock a dope fiend's socks off." Rubio emphasized his words.

"Twenty-six? Come on now, Rubio. I'm spending two hundred thousand dollars off the top. Work with me. How about twenty-four?" Paulie countered, trying to get as close as he could to Johansen's price.

Rubio rubbed his hands over his slick, bald head. "Two hundred thousand dollars you say? My last customer spent seven hundred thousand up front, and that was a small order. Paulie, you got to look at I'm using all of my resources and manpower to get this stuff to your doorstep and this is cheap... only because I like you. The only way I can give you that kind of price is if you handle your own shipping. That's the best I can do," Rubio said, then looked up at the waitress who was heading their way.

"Hi, I'm Amy. Are you gentlemen ready to order?" the tall, lanky blonde asked with a big smile stretched across her face.

"Yes, give me the filet, rare, with Lyonnaise Potatoes and Spinach au Gratin," Rubio ordered, while Paulie looked over the menu.

"Give me the same, but make mine medium-well," Paulie told her. As he laid down the menu, he thought about how good the food sounded. Things had been so crazy lately, he couldn't remember the last time he sat back and ate a good meal.

"Drinks?" the waitress asked.

"Give us a bottle of the best champagne you have in the back so we can celebrate new business ventures," Rubio announced.

Paulie smiled in agreement, then waited for the waitress to walk off before he spoke.

"Guess twenty-six it is. How do you want the money?" Paulie asked, ready to put things in motion.

"Cash!" Rubio said, then burst into laughter like he had just said the funniest thing in the world.

"Ha! Rubio, you got me!" Playing along, Paulie faked his laugh.

As fast as the laughter started, it stopped.

Rubio looked directly in Paulie's eyes as he spoke. "I have people up your way. You need to call them as soon as you get back. They will tell you to bring your car out to be repaired and will give you directions. Have the money in the trunk. They will pull your car in the garage and tell you to come back in a couple of hours. You leave and come back in three hours. Take a taxi and grab lunch or some shit. When you pick up your ride, everything will be in place. You are the only person who can do this pick up...only you. If you decide on a driver afterwards, cool, but only you enter and exit that garage," Rubio explained in a firm tone.

Just then, the waitress returned with the champagne, and a short while later, their meals arrived as well.

They engaged in small talk as they ate and sipped on the expensive champagne. Paulie, not much of a drinker, was on his second glass, while Rubio was finishing his fifth. After Rubio polished off the rest of the bottle, they called it a night.

"I'll be in touch. Have a safe trip, my friend." Rubio slurred as he crossed the lot to the beautiful Cadillac.

"A'ight, drive safe," Paulie replied.

Looking at his watch, he saw it was close to nine o'clock. He then looked at his phone, knowing Sashay would be calling him any minute.

TONY STORY

CHAPTER 24

G STREET CHRONICLES
~A NEW URBAN DYNASTY~

WWW.GSTREETCHRONICLES.COM

LB and Loon sat around Loon's apartment until the sun disappeared behind the horizon and the moon made its entrance into the night. They had plans to hit the city looking for Paulie. Walking outside while puffing on the blunt of sticky, they jumped in Loon's old-school Chevy ready to hit the streets. Loon laid his .45 automatic on the seat and stuck his key into the car's ignition.

Click! Click! Click!

He turned the key over and over again, but got the same results.

"Fuck! Shit won't start!" Loon spat, slapping the steering wheel as LB hit the blunt hard and passed it to him.

"Damn, my nigga, we stuck like chuck," LB added. He held in the smoke from his last toke until he made himself have a coughing fit.

"Fuck that!" Loon said, pulling the keys from the ignition. He got out and walked around to the trunk.

Popping the trunk open with a turn of the key, Loon didn't

waste time getting what he was looking for out of the trunk. He grabbed a flat-head screwdriver, a pair of grip pliers, and a small hammer. Before Loon closed the trunk, LB was out of the car and standing next to him, waiting for the blunt he had between his lips.

"Nigga, what? You planning on fixing this bitch?" LB asked, looking down at the tools Loon held.

"Hell naw, nigga! We 'bout to grab us another ride!" Loon told him, as he pulled the blunt hard twice and then passed it back to LB.

* * * * *

Paulie looked at the time and saw it was nine o'clock. He was sitting in the downtown traffic waiting on the light to change, when his cell phone rang. He looked at the screen and saw it was Sashay calling.

"Damn, she sure ain't the play-hard-to-get type. She don't put no cut on her objective. She's calling at nine o'clock on the dot." He laughed before answering.

"Hello?"

"Hey, what's up? You ready to hang out with me yet?" Sashay asked seductively, as she stood in front of her bathroom mirror fixing her eyeliner and lip gloss.

"Are you ready to hang with me is the question?" Paulie replied, reversing her question on her.

"You know I am, sexy. You going to show me a good time before you go home?" Sashay asked, then she poked out her lips and removed the excess lip gloss.

"Fa' sho. I just ate, but if you're hungry, we can grab a bite to eat. If not, let's go to the comedy club. I make it my business to hit it every time I visit Atlanta. Them niggas be straight tripping." Paulie pulled off into the night traffic.

"I'm good on the grub. I just ate too. So, we can just snack on something at the comedy club. How about I meet you there in thirty minutes?" she suggested.

Exiting the bathroom, she grabbed her mini skirt and deep-cut blouse she had laid out for the night.

"I'll be there," Paulie replied, anxiously waiting to have his way with the fine, petite Sashay.

* * * * *

LB and Loon walked discreetly through the grocery store parking lot located two blocks from Loon's place. Looking from ride to ride, they spotted a Chevy Monte Carlo. They looked at each other and smiled, knowing it would be an easy peel. Ducking low, they eased over to the car and tried the door handle.

"Bingo!" LB said.

He pulled the passenger side door open, climbed in, and then reached over to unlock the driver side door so Loon could get in. He pulled his .9mm from his waist and readied it just in case the owner of the car showed up. LB kept watch while Loon went to work with the hammer and screwdriver. In two minutes flat, the car's engine came to life.

"The ghetto!" *Boom! Boom! Boom! Boom! Boom!*

The twelve-inch woofers scared both of them. They grabbed for the radio buttons at the same time, trying to turn down the Too Short song blasting from the car's premium sound system.

"Damn! Let's go!" LB called out after he killed the volume

on the car stereo.

He ducked down low in the seat while Loon guided the stolen car out of the parking lot and into the busy street.

"Fire on up, nigga!" Loon told LB, as he made a right and headed to the known ballers' nightspot where he hoped to find Paulie.

* * * * *

Paulie pulled up at the comedy club and sat in the car waiting for Sashay to show up. He took in all of the skimpily-dressed, beautiful women that were with their high-rolling escorts. Paulie had thought about relocating a couple years ago, but decided against it. Back in Atlanta again and still loving it, he thought about reconsidering. It was just something about Philly that just wouldn't let him leave.

He bobbed his head to Drake's new single and patiently waited on Sashay. Ten minutes later, he saw a bright yellow Mercedes CLK pull into the parking lot. Seconds later, he set eyes on Sashay, who was stuffed in a mini skirt that left nothing to the imagination and a top that displayed her cleavage. Paulie found himself already crazy about the down south sista.

He stepped out of his rental and met her as she crossed the lot, walking in his direction.

"Um um um…bangin'." Paulie looked her up and down, shaking his head side to side as he approached her.

"I'm digging what I'm seeing too." She smiled and wrapped her small arm around his waist.

They walked up to the door hugged up like a couple who had been together for years. Paulie paid the lady at the door, and they entered the dimly lit club looking for a good table. Paulie made sure he didn't get too close to the stage, because when comedians get low on jokes, they always go for the patrons sitting the closest to the stage to pick on. Paulie chose a table off to the side, but a good distance to the stage.

"This shit's about to be crazy. What are you drinking?" Paulie asked, catching Sashay staring at him.

"It doesn't matter. Whatever you order," Sashay told him, while taking in the good rugged looks of the man with the sexy, northern swag.

As Paulie raised his hand to get the waiter's attention, Sashay discreetly checked out the diamonds he wore around his neck and both wrists. They twinkled in the dimly lit room.

"Hi. May I help you?" the young, attractive, dark skin waitress asked, while making it obvious that she was checking Paulie out.

Sashay gave her a death stare and rolled her eyes as Paulie ordered.

"Yes, could you give us two Cirocs with pineapple juice and light ice?" Paulie told the waitress, as Sashay tried her best not to blast the disrespectful waitress.

Before the night was over, they had drank four rounds, eaten two chicken finger baskets, and laughed until they cried. Paulie was having a wonderful time, something he hadn't had the pleasure of doing in a while. It felt good to him not having to dodge bullets and watch his back. Not that he had let his guard down on the streets; he just didn't have to hold them so far up while away.

"I really enjoyed this. What's next?" Sashay asked, feeling the effects of the alcohol as they exited the club behind patrons who were still laughing.

"You," Paulie replied. He was also reeling off the Ciroc, but he meant what he said literally.

"Ummm, sounds good and freaky," Sashay replied. She felt the wetness increase between her legs.

"Let's go to my hotel and get to know each other a little better," Paulie slightly slurred.

He wrapped his arm around her while planting small kisses on her neck. The alcohol had them both hot, and the only thing that would calm the two fires was some intense thrusting and a hard orgasm.

"Okay, I'll follow you. What's the room number, just in case we get separated in traffic? I got to make a pit stop by the gas station too," Sashay said, as she broke the embrace and headed to the car.

"Room 312," Paulie told her.

He opened the door to his rental and climbed behind the wheel. Paulie was feeling good. He had secured him another connect and was now about to get knee deep in some ATL pussy. No guns blasting, no ducking, no violence. Just big money deals and some good sex. He smiled as he pulled out of the parking lot.

When he entered the hotel's parking lot, he was surprised to see Sashay pulling up a couple minutes behind him since she said she had to stop for gas. They parked a couple cars apart and walked hand-in-hand up to the room.

"I love this hotel. I want to do it so everybody can see," Sashay said playfully, while grabbing his belt buckle as they rode in the glass elevator that gave patrons a view of the city.

"A'ight now, girl," Paulie said, reaching over and taking her into his arms.

It felt as if he'd known Sashay forever, but the reality of it was he hadn't known her twenty-four hours. Still, he was feeling her deeply. He tried to figure out what had him tripping over a woman he'd just met, and he couldn't blame it on the alcohol.

Exiting the elevator, they made their way to his room. Paulie pulled out the key and opened the door.

"Nice," Sashay said, following Paulie into the room.

Before he could close the door, Sashay was all over him.

"Hold up," Paulie told her as he locked the room door.

"Damn, baby. Fuck yeah," Sashay cooed as she resumed her act of undressing Paulie.

When he was totally naked, she stepped back and admired his cut frame, six-pack, and bulging muscles. She didn't waste any time stripping down to her birthday suit. Paulie was amazed by the beauty of the woman who stood before him. He had been with many women in his time, and still, Sashay had the most banging body he had ever come across. She was blemish free, flawless, and well-defined in all the right places.

He laid back on the bed and she climbed in with him.

* * * * *

LB and Loon pulled into Club City Lights' parking lot looking for any signs of Paulie.

"Man, it's going to be hard as hell trying to find this nigga out here. Ain't no telling which one of his whips he's in. Then finding one of 'em is going to be crazy 'cause everything out this bitch is sitting on chrome and exotic," Loon stated, as they cruised up and down the rows of cars looking for Paulie's ride.

"We going to find this nigga if he out here," LB said, tapping the ashes off the blunt onto the floor of the stolen car.

"Ain't that the nigga Trell who used to be with Ty and them? He probably know where that nigga Paulie at," Loon said as he pulled up beside Trell, who was standing outside of his snow-white Range Rover that sparkled in the night, talking on his cell phone.

"Hold on," Trell said into the phone as he grabbed for his pistol. He quickly realized he'd left it in the truck.

He eased back, cursing himself for being caught slipping.

Seeing the man was about to make a move, LB called out, "Yo, Trell!"

Trell calmed down a little after hearing his name called. He stepped from the side of his truck, squinting as he tried to see who this person was calling his name.

"Where that boy Paulie at?" Loon called out from the driver seat.

Getting a good look inside the car, Trell saw it was the two young, wild niggas; Loon and LB. Aware that LB was still a wanted man, he played it cool, looking to help silence the young, out-of-control nigga.

"Man, what y'all niggas up to? Paulie on his way out here. We 'bout to put on for our city tonight! Y'all niggas too young to get in this bitch. Oh! I can holla at my man Rob. He can get y'all in," Trell lied, trying to see what the young niggas next move would be.

"Naw, we good. We'll just lay back and wait for him," LB said.

Trell looked over in the car at the automatic weapons lying on the seat.

"Y'all boys can come on in now," Trell said, again playing it off.

Neither replied as they pulled off to the side of the lot. As soon as they were out of view, Trell lifted his phone to his ear and realized Monica was still on the line bitching about him not coming over.

"You never want us to—"

Click!

He hung up on her and called Paulie, but got no answer. Looking around to make sure the young niggas were still out of sight, he called Man-Man, Paulie's stand-up guy who was also on the hunt for the young LB.

* * * * *

"Mmmm," Sashay moaned while sucking on Paulie's hard erection like it was her favorite flavored Popsicle.

"Shit!" Paulie groaned.

She handled his stick like a pro. He laid back and enjoyed the performance.

After performing every trick in the book with her mouth on his dick, she straddled him. Paulie was in a zone. He didn't know if it was the alcohol or his lust that made him disregard the condom tucked in his wallet. Sashay didn't think twice as she slid down on his throbbing wood.

"Ahh fuck!" she moaned.

She wiggled down on it, adjusting to its length. As soon as she was comfortable perched on top of him, she started moving to his rhythm.

Paulie clawed her ass and then spread it apart, making sure he got every inch of his manhood inside her as she rode him hard.

"Oh, shit yeah!" he called out.

She lifted up and reversed her position without him even having to pull out.

Sashay rocked back and forth while holding on to his kneecaps for balance.

Smack! Smack! Smack!

Her ass slapped against his thighs louder as more sweat formed between them. Paulie reached up and stopped her midstroke. She slowly turned around and looked at him, wondering why he stopped her.

"Lay down," he told her, lifting her off him.

He gently squeezed her firm C-cups while taking one into his mouth and sucking on her erect nipple. She moaned in ecstasy as he nursed on her breast like a newborn baby. After showing each nipple equal attention, he opened her legs and slowly slid his dick in. Her moans of pain and pleasure aroused Paulie even more. She wrapped her legs around his waist tight as he dove in. He didn't pound her hard; he long stroked her slow and steady as she held him tight, calling out his name.

"Oh my lawd! Yes, Paulie!"

She screamed so loud that they couldn't hear the person fumbling with the hotel room door trying to gain entrance.

* * * * *

"What kind of car them niggas in, bruh?" Man-Man asked as he rushed out of his apartment and got in his late-model Tahoe.

"They riding in a blue Monte Carlo with tinted windows. You'll see it 'cause it's the raggediest shit out here. Be careful, 'cause them lil' niggas packing much heat. I'm about to bounce off in this spot. Just hit me up if you need me," Trell told Man-Man, who was already en route to the club.

"That's real, fam. I got these suckers. These lil' bitches gonna learn tonight," Man-Man said, then clicked off the line and fired up a Newport.

LB and Loon pulled off to the side of the lot where they could have a full view of everybody who stood in line waiting to enter the club. They rambled through the CDs that were in a plastic grocery bag in the backseat until they ran across Flamers, one of Meek Mill's first hits. They popped it in, fired up a blunt, and waited patiently for Paulie to show.

"Damn, I gotta piss," LB said as Loon rapped along with the song and pulled on the blunt.

"This nigga need to bring his ass on," Loon said.

LB opened his door and got out to piss. He rounded the building out of sight because he didn't need Philly's finest hauling him off to jail for indecent exposure or trespassing. Just as he was taking a leak, Man-Man turned into the lot.

The AR-15 on his passenger seat was loaded, cocked, and ready to blast. It didn't take him long to spot the blue tinted-out Monte Carlo sitting off in the far corner of the lot. He killed his lights and cruised slowly through the lot until he was a few feet away from the Monte Carlo. Loon sat rapping to the Meek Mill's joint and smoking the blunt while watching the clubgoers going in and out. He never noticed Man-Man easing out of the Tahoe with the AR-15 in his grip.

Man-Man got in range, lifted the AR-15, and pulled the trigger. Fire shot out the barrel as it let loose.

Plat! Plat! Plat! Plat!

The sound of the bullets hitting the car let you know they

were penetrating the metal with ease.

"Oh shit!" LB screamed as he fumbled to tuck his limp wood back in his pants, then struck out running.

"Ahhhh!" Loon's screams could be heard a mile away as the AR-15 chopped him and the car up.

The club's patrons screamed and ran for cover as the shots lit up the parking lot. The people in the club didn't even realize a murder was taking place outside, something that had become a regular occurrence in the city of Philly.

After emptying the clip, Man-Man calmly turned, walked back over to his Tahoe, and got in. As he slowly pulled off, he noticed a figure in the distance running full speed away from the club. Man-Man grabbed the half-smoked Newport out of his ashtray and fired it up as he blended in with the frantic people speeding away from the scene.

* * * * *

After trying the door for a third time, Shawty got mad and stormed off, but not before hearing Sashay moaning and screaming Paulie's name.

"Stupid-ass bitch!" he spat as he walked away. He made sure the pistol was secure in his waist so it wouldn't be noticed when he walked by hotel security.

"Fuck this pussy, Paulie! Give me that dick! Yes! Oh shhh… yes!" Sashay screamed, digging her freshly manicured nails in his back.

Like a possessed madman, Paulie pumped faster and faster while looking down at the pretty Sashay. Her fuck faces had him going all out. He almost got lost in the moment and told her that he loved her as he stiffened up and shot his warm juices inside of her.

"I…Oh, Paulie! Oh damn, I'm coming!" she called out. Sashay grabbed him tight and sped up the pace until she was shaking violently. "Oh my…God!"

"Damn, baby, you a fuckin' beast," Paulie told her after rolling off of her and trying to catch his breath.

"Naw, baby, you the beast." Sashay told him.

She wondered why Shawty hadn't showed up. Then she remembered Paulie had locked the door.

"Shit!" she shouted as she jumped up, then caught herself.

"What up? You good?" Paulie asked, watching as she quickly climbed out of bed.

"I'm good, baby. I got to pee pee," she lied.

Before heading to the bathroom, she discreetly grabbed her cell phone off the floor next to her skirt.

Woozy from the liquor and tired from the day's events, Paulie laid back. It didn't take him but a minute to doze off. The last thing he heard was Sashay flushing the toilet and running water.

Sashay quickly dialed Shawty's number.

"Bitch, what kind of games you playing! Why the fuck the door locked?" Shawty cursed. He had been pacing back and forth in the downstairs lobby waiting to hear from her.

"Nigga, I didn't know he locked the door. I'm opening it now," Sashay said lowly through clenched teeth.

She hung up and stepped out of the bathroom. When she noticed Paulie lightly snoring, she was relieved. She wouldn't have to make an excuse to get to the door now. She crept across the room and quietly cracked the door, then grabbed her clothes off the floor and put them on. By the time she had fully dressed,

Shawty was creeping into the room. Sashay could tell by the look in her baby daddy's eyes that he was angry, so she hurriedly slid past him and out the door. Shawty made sure the door was closed before drawing his gun.

"Say, shawty, don't move. Just be easy and come out that shit," Shawty said, jarring Paulie out of his sleep.

Paulie's eyes shot open. He blinked twice, hoping the man standing over him with the gun in his face was just a dream. A few seconds later, he realized he wasn't dreaming.

"Fuck! Okay, my nigga, you got it. Just don't pull the trigger," Paulie said calmly as he started taking off his jewels and handing them over to the man.

He looked around for Sashay, but already knew what it was. Shawty picked up on Paulie looking for her and shook his head.

"Pussy get a nigga every time," Shawty stated as Paulie handed over all of his pieces.

Shawty took a quick glance at the pieces and knew they had hit the jackpot.

"Put the cover over yo' head, nigga," Shawty ordered, while stuffing the jewelry in his pocket.

"Man, if you going to kill me, do it while looking at me, dawg. I ain't about to cover my head," Paulie snapped, ready to die.

"Bitch nigga, when Shawty tell you to do something, do it! Feel me!" Shawty growled as he brought the pistol down across Paulie's head, dazing him.

Shawty took this time to bolt from the room. By the time Paulie shook off the dizziness, Shawty was long gone.

* * * * *

Later that night, Shawty walked into the condo that he and Sashay shared, still pissed that Sashay had enjoyed fucking the man she had set up.

"I heard you screaming and shit! Don't fuckin' lie to me!" Shawty screamed as Sashay sat on the bed crying.

After hearing him out, she started screaming back.

"I didn't enjoy shit! I do all this shit for your ass! I hate all this shit! I swear I do!" Sashay lied as she wiped her tears. She secretly wished she had kept her mouth closed about Paulie in the beginning and made him her out-of-town side piece.

Shawty loved his baby mama. He had a soft spot for her because she was a real ride-or-die chick when they were low on cash. Feeling bad for scolding her so viciously, he walked over, took her into his arms, and brought his mouth down to hers for a kiss, but she stopped him.

"No. I need to rinse out my mouth and brush first." As soon as she spoke those words, her hand flew up to her mouth. She knew she had fucked up.

Shawty couldn't believe it. Sashay had never gone down on a lick before. His temperature went from 0 to 100 in seconds.

"You sucked…" Shawty stopped mid-sentence; he knew for sure that she had enjoyed her time with Paulie.

Sashay was at a loss for words, but she anticipated the beating Shawty gave her throughout the remainder of the night.

G STREET CHRONICLES
A NEW URBAN DYNASTY

WWW.GSTREETCHRONICLES.COM

TONY STORY

CHAPTER 25

G STREET CHRONICLES
A NEW URBAN DYNASTY

WWW.GSTREETCHRONICLES.COM

"**B**itch nigga…fuck-ass nigga…hoe nigga! That's on Tony, nigga! I'm deading you, nigga!" LB seethed as he walked through his spot.

He cursed and fumed all the way home the prior night, knowing another one of his friends had lost his life to the streets. He knew Mikey wouldn't be seeing daylight for some time because he was already on papers. Now his man Loon was laid up lifeless in a deep freezer waiting to be identified.

"I swear, nigga, I ain't stopping 'til I dead yo' ass!" LB screamed as he walked over to his closet and pulled out every gun he owned.

After taking an inventory of his fire power, he grabbed his cell phone off the kitchen table and started calling everybody he knew who could possibly help him find Paulie. He got lucky after the third call.

"Boy, that's on God, fam. I got you. Whatever you need me fo'?" LB told Yella, one of Tony's old friends who just so happened to know the vicinity of Paulie's crib.

"No need, young'in. I fucked with ya brother hard. Just

make sure you handle that nigga the right way," Yella told him with a smirk on his face, glad his competition was about to be eliminated.

"You know I am. Mannn, this shit straight up for bro," LB said, missing his brother.

"Keep me posted, lil' bro," Yella told him before they hung up.

LB looked at the paper in his hand with directions on it to Paulie's upscale neighborhood and smiled a devious smile.

* * * * *

Paulie touched the lump on his head and winced in pain. He had taken three Excedrin hoping his splitting headache would subside. He cursed himself again and again for being so careless. He rubbed his hands across the place where his jewels use to hang. He felt naked without his pieces.

As he walked through the airport, he made a mental note to hit up Shyne's Jeweler for some bigger, nicer pieces. He pulled out his phone and made a call before he boarded.

"The number you have reached, 404-344…"

Paulie knew before he even keyed in the number that it would be disconnected. He shook his head in disgust, hating that he had let the down south, country freak slither up under him without detection. He gave her, her props, though. She was good at what she did, actually like a pro.

During the flight, Paulie made mental notes, initiating his plan: call Rubio, get the drop situated, connect with all of his clientele to let them know shop was back open, and last but not least, find the young LB and wipe him the fuck out. Paulie was tired of playing chicken with the menace, so he decided to put a bigger check on LB's head and at the same time hit the streets himself. He knew by doing this, one way or the other, the nigga wouldn't live to see Sunday. Paulie knew fifty thousand dollars on the nigga wouldn't give him long to live, so he deducted that from his stash.

He arrived back in Philly a little under two hours later. Exiting the terminal, he caught the shuttle to the Park & Ride to retrieve his car. Glad to be back in the city, he got behind the wheel of his Maserati, turned up the Jim Jones playing on the radio, and whipped out the lot, heading back to the hood. He ran his hand over the shrinking lump on his head once again.

"Fuck ATL!" he yelled as he thought about Sashay and his pieces.

TONY STORY

CHAPTER 26

MAKING ENDS MEET
TWO DAYS LATER

G STREET CHRONICLES
~A NEW URBAN DYNASTY~

WWW.GSTREETCHRONICLES.COM

The city was cold, but gunners around the city were bringing the heat. The murder rate since Ty's death had almost
doubled from last year, and city officials were calling it "a
war in the streets".

Even though bodies were dropping left and right, hustlers
and d-boys were not letting up. They continued to make ends
meet in the street. LB was on high alert because he had gotten
word that Paulie had fifty-thousand on his head and a couple
niggas from around the way were lurking, looking to collect. LB
didn't panic one bit though. He just kept his heat close and ready.

Paulie was back in full swing, getting off birdies left and right.
Niggas all over Philly loved not only the product, but the prices
too.

"When you jump them, just get right back at me. Don't be
bullshitting, 'cause this shit going fast," Paulie told Gump, one
of his biggest-spending customers.

Gump moved blocks like niggas in the trap moved rocks.

"That's the word, money! P-man, your shit is crazy fire. My

niggas say the cluckers loving this shit. I'll hit you tomorrow after I get with my people from Delaware," Gump said, then hopped back in his Camaro and pulled out the gas station.

Paulie had the city on smash. Rubio's people had come through like clockwork, and Rubio had lived up to his word on giving him the best product around that could be stepped on a couple times. Paulie was surprised when he took one block, and after almost doubling it, the product was still high-grade quality. Paulie knew that dealing with the quality of dope he was getting, it wouldn't be long before he was stacking seven figures.

"Meet me at the gas station on the corner of Haines and Stenton," Paulie told Cody, one of his other big spenders who was looking to buy four birds.

"Ten-four, nigga. Just make sure you show love this time," Cody joked, knowing the price and quality were well worth what he was paying.

"Yeah, I hear ya." Paulie laughed as he laid his phone inside the console and put his Bentley GT in drive, pulling out the gas station.

After serving Cody, he confirmed his meeting with the jeweler to check out some new pieces.

"I'll be there at five o'clock. Is that good?" Paulie asked, stuffing the money from the two sales under his passenger seat.

"No problem, Mr. Paulie. I have some nice pieces that are going to light up your life," Shyne joked, knowing the young black hustlers and entertainers loved bling.

Paulie was riding high. The whole city had his back. Niggas were out like the Feds trying to find the lil' nigga LB to off him. It seemed like he had fallen off the face of the earth. Paulie had even turned a few blocks himself looking for him. Things were quiet...a little too quiet...and Paulie didn't like that.

After turning a few more blocks checking trap, he headed to Shyne's Jeweler to see what they had for him. As soon as he hit the door of the jeweler, he set eyes on Big Lou, one of his old hustling buddies from way back who had relocated to New York. Last he heard, Big Lou was doing it big in the entertainment business. He was one of the biggest promoters in the Big Apple, and when Paulie took in his taste of clothes and jewelry, he could tell he was definitely doing pretty good.

"Paulie, my boy!" Big Lou wheezed, greeting his old buddy.

"Boy, what it do? Man, Big Lou, what up?" Paulie called out excitedly as he crossed the floor, glad to see his old friend who he hadn't seen in years.

"Young P, I see you still shining like a diamond. You eating good, boy!" Big Lou commented, taking Paulie in a half hug.

The woman behind the counter waited patiently while holding the iced-out watch they had just added links to so it would fit around the big man's wrist.

"I ain't doing nothing but trying to survive, big homie. Nigga, I see you getting it yourself. That there had to run you a car, and I ain't talking about the monthly payments," Paulie joked, looking at the watch that had to have cost at least thirty stacks or more.

"Ha! Boy, you still got jokes! You know I like nice shit. You know I'm like that boy Biggie...fat, black, and ugly as ever, but however!" Big Lou laughed, then handed the woman behind the counter his credit card so she could charge the sale.

"You crazy, boy." Paulie laughed as they slapped five.

"Excuse me, Mr. Paulie. Please come with me so I can show you the nice pieces I told you about," said the man, who was the jeweler to all the big spenders in the city and surrounding cities.

"Damn, big baller, you get your shit from the back? If I had your hands, I'd throw these bitches away," Big Lou joked, holding out his hands and displaying the five-carat diamond ring that lit up the room even in the bright sunlight.

"Yeah, I hear ya...and see ya," Paulie replied before stepping through the counter's swinging door and heading to the back.

"Say, I almost forgot! I got that boy Meek Mill and his Dream Chasers crew at club Whispers tonight. You need to fall through. It's going to be crazy! Just ask for me at the door. Better yet, just call me when you get outside," Big Lou told Paulie. He reached in his pocket, pulled out a business card, and handed it to him.

"Bet! I'll be out there," Paulie replied, taking the card and sticking it in his back pocket.

Big Lou exited the store, and Paulie went to check out his new pieces.

Thirty minutes later, Paulie was walking out with an iced-out watch, an iced-out platinum chain, a four-inch wide diamond bracelet, and a three-carat rock on his hand.

"I'm back, bitches!" Paulie called out as he left the store after handing over half of what he had made off that day's drops.

* * * * *

LB rode through Paulie's hood for the fifth time in two days. He knew for sure he was in Paulie's neck of the woods, but just didn't know his exact address. He looked for any one of Paulie's cars or any car that could have been his. Soon, LB came to a fast conclusion that it was no use because every driveway in the upscale neighborhood had a nice whip sitting on chrome out front, and the garages that were open boasted the same luxury vehicles.

He made one last round, and just as he was making his way out of the neighborhood, a particular house caught his attention. Not so much the house, but the car in the house's driveway with a customized tag that read *P-City*. The Benz was an emerald green with what looked like 24-inch Lexani rims. LB stopped across the street from the house and surveyed the scene. He could tell no one was home because the porch light was still on and every room he could see from his view was dark. He tucked his .9mm and got out the car. He walked over to the garage like he lived there and looked in. He knew that was Paulie's crib. The metallic blue Audi R-8 had been the talk of the streets when he first came through in it. LB knew he finally had the right house.

LB tried to open the garage door. After having no luck, he climbed the porch and tried the front door. Still couldn't gain entry. Giving up, he walked back down the front porch steps, looked back, and smiled.

"Nigga, I got yo' ass now," he said to himself.

Then he got back behind the wheel of his Chevy and pulled off with big plans of returning.

TONY STORY

CHAPTER 27

G STREET CHRONICLES
~A NEW URBAN DYNASTY~

WWW.GSTREETCHRONICLES.COM

The line outside of Whispers stretched almost a half mile long. Hustlers, players, and some of the baddest females from the city and surrounding cities were trying to get in to see one of Philly's own, who had made it out the hood and was topping the charts. Meek Mill, Louie V Gutta, Lil Snupe and the rest of Dream Chasers crew had the house packed.

Considering it to be a special night, Paulie pulled out his prize possession, his Audi A-8, for the special occasion. As he cruised through the city, he had people pointing and turning their heads like he was a famous celebrity or sports figure. Paulie felt good. He felt like money, he looked like money, and he let it show as he cruised along. He was pretty sure he would bump into a lot of other hustlers and players around the city, so he made sure his new pieces were sitting just right. He wanted to make sure that before the night was over, all of Philly knew who the man was in the streets.

He whipped into the parking lot, pulled up alongside the long line of Meek Mill fans, and waited for the valet to come retrieve his vehicle.

"Be careful with this one here," he told the valet, while handing over his keys.

When he stepped out the car, he felt every eye in the line on him. He never even looked over to see if his assumptions were correct. He just adjusted his watch, which was slightly off center, and stepped off, heading to the front where he stopped and pulled out his cell phone.

Not even five minutes later, Big Lou's assistant was at the door waving Paulie in. People in the line checked out the VIP treatment he was getting, especially the women. They made it their business to remember the very important player.

When Paulie stepped in the spot, he instantly picked up on the Philly vibe. He entered the packed club and looked left to right, noticing all of the big and small time hustlers and d-boys in attendance.

"Come up here. Big Lou is expecting you," the male assistant said as they cut through the crowd, heading to the club's VIP area.

"Boy, you made it! Come on over here!" Big Lou bellowed, motioning for Paulie to join him and the group of video vixens he had invited out for the show.

"Nigga, pay homage!" a familiar voice called out from behind him.

Paulie turned around and dapped up his good friend and fellow hustler, Trell.

"Y'all two rich niggas in the same spot? Damn, I don't stand a chance!" Paulie said jokingly over the Lil' Wayne blasting from the club's sound system.

"Good to see you too, bro. You holla at Man-Man?" Trell

asked, getting serious.

"Naw, but I saw he called. I got to hit him back," Paulie replied, wondering what was going on with his young partner Man-Man.

Trell leaned over and whispered to him, "He had put in some work on the lil' nigga LB, but when the smoke cleared, it was his homeboy that got hit up. Make sure you get at him. He'll tell you about it. The funny part is the two lil' niggas pulled up on me looking for you. These lil' stupid-ass young niggas playing a game and don't even know who team muthafuckers play on."

Trell laughed as Paulie nodded his head in approval.

"That nigga gonna be handled soon, trust me," Paulie assured Trell, who was already aware of the fifty-thousand dollars on the lil' nigga's head.

"I already know," Trell said and smiled, as they joined Big Lou and the group of vixens who were up drinking and dancing.

As the night went on, Paulie ran into Gump, Cody, and a lot of his other clientele from the city. He partied hard like there was no tomorrow.

Suddenly, the lights started blinking like crazy and the music stopped.

"What the hell?" Paulie said, looking around.

"Boy, just chill. My nigga 'bout to fire this bitch up," Big Lou said, holding a bottle of Ciroc while smiling and facing the stage.

The whole club's attention turned toward the bright spotlight jetting around the room. It trickled for about two minutes before stopping on the man of the house. Holding the microphone, Meek Mill stood illuminated in the spotlight as he looked out over the crowd. Paulie vaguely remembered the young star from the old hood, but knew his name well.

"Man, where the hoes at? That nigga ain't talkin' 'bout nothin,'" a young hustler from the same block Meek grew up on mumbled to his other partner, who really was an undercover Meek Mill fan. His friend kept his love for Meek Mill hidden when rolling with his man because he always hated on this man who rose up out these streets and became a star.

The crowd went wild when the lights focused on Meek Mill. When the beat from one of his hits from the first Dream Chasers mixtape dropped, the crowd went wild.

> *This is the life*
> *This is the life*
> *Yea, this is the life*
> *This is the life*
>
> *Tony killed his own man Ty for a whole brick*
> *Lined him all up and gave him the whole clip*
> *Said he wasn't eatin', he wanted his own shit*
> *And not to mention Ty was fuckin' his old bitch*
> *But Ty wasn't a shooter, that nigga just sold bricks*
> *And Tony, he was reckless; he never had no picks*
> *Tony was like the Alpo, Ty was the Lil' Rich*
> *Two niggas with a dream that plotted on goin' rich*
> *Started as a team, but Ty, he got on quick*
> *Jealousy the reason that Ty got left all stiff*
> *Got Tony at the viewing, Ty mom crying to him*
> *He hug her; he tell her whoever did this, he gonna do 'em*
> *From there, it was a silence; she ain't condone violence*
> *But they killed her only son, so when he said it, she just nodded*
> *And he told her that he got her; Grimy at its best*

TONY STORY

Like Tony had a cold, he feelin' slimy in his chest
Yes, he had the nerve to carry the casket
Strapped up before he went, he had to carry his ratchet
He nervous, walkin' like he tryna carry him faster
Nigga even grabbed the shovel tried to bury him faster

Next week he at the mall, Rollie on his arm
Two bad bitches with him, laughing, having a ball
Seen Ty cousin Paul; Paul couldn't believe it
Same nigga asked him for a front last weekend
Walkin' 'round the mall, Louie on, bags Neiman
With the gold-diggin' bitches Lil' Kee and Bad Trina
He dapped Tony up, tryna cap Tony up
In his head thinkin' how he gonna clap Tony up
But Tony he ain't worried, 'cause he strapped Tony up
Seven days of running he already turned it up
He got Paulie burnin' up, he ready to ride
He know Tony a killer, but he ready to die
Ahhhhh, smell the death all in the air
Paulie thinkin' 'bout puttin' a check all on his head, but he can't
'Cause Tony he done killed his first cousin
If he let somebody else do it, it won't mean nothin'
He wanna see him bleedin', he wanna see him gaspin'
Wanna watch him die slow, like he sufferin' from cancer
Feel that Tony did it, but he don't really know the answer
So he gonna let it burn until he get confirmed

Couple months fly by, Tony on the high rise
Started flippin', now he got them chickens in like Popeye's
Paulie still gettin' it, always been a top guy

He ain't really club, but tonight, he gonna stop by
Seen Lil' Kee and them, it was two or three of them
Standin' in the line; he said, "I'mma pay for me and them"
Pulled his money out, started countin' it, and teasin' 'em
You know Kee gold-diggin' ass just wanna be with him
Slid up in the club, told the waiter, "Give me three of 'em"
Bottles of the Spade, now Kee just wanna leave with him
He said, "Where yo phone at"; she said, "Where you goin' at?"
He said, "I'ma slide out"; she said, "I'mma ride out"
Told her friends "Call y'all tomorrow when I get to my mom house"
They got right up out of there, took her to his side house
Soon as they got in the crib, she just blew his mind out
Wasted off them bottles Paulie bought, she on her nod out

But Paulie, he ain't goin' to sleep
Grab her phone up off the sheets
Took it to the living room, her messages he goin' through
Scroll up to Tony name, he text her "What you doin', boo?"
She text him back, "I'm in the crib"; he text her back, "You comin'
through?"
She text, "Where I'm comin' to?"; he text back
"1022 Woodstock in North Philly, take the E-Way to the zoo"
She text back, "I'm comin' now"; lookie here what Paulie found
Got the drop on Tony where he living and its goin' down

Couple weeks later, Paulie on Woodstock
Sittin' in the minivan, tinted with his hood cocked
Tony just rode up, Paulie got the good drop
.44 in his hand 'bout to make the hood rock
Tony slippin', Paulie all dippin'

Walk'd up on his car like "What's poppin', lil' nigga?"
Tony lookin' shocked, his Glock was in his box
So he couldn't grab for it; Paul said, "That's yo' ass, boy"
He said, "You still need that work that you asked for?"
Dropped it all on his lap; it was four and a half raw
Tony he lookin 'crazy; he know that's his last straw
And Paulie just let it go, put his brains on the dashboard
POW!

After he finished spitting Part 1 of *The Tony Story*, the lights went back off again and a simulated blast went off on stage. When the lights came back on, Meek stood with a black hoodie pulled over his head. He held his head low until the beat shook the club. He slowly lifted his head with the look of murder in his eyes and went in on Part 2...

Paulie killed Tony right and Tony killed Ty, so it was only right
Bring 'em back twenty years, they was homies, tight
Sixth grade, for the love of the paper ain't nothing nice
And Paulie just loving life
He got them birds and he serving niggas left and right
Never used to party in them clubs every night
Popping bottles, blowing paper
Balling hard, he know they hating
But they gon' respect it, 'cause he rocked Tony
And Tony had the hood on smash by his lonely
And Paulie getting money, so them bitches all on him
And his young boys riding, they ready to fall for him
'Cause word on the street that Paulie did that
Used Kee gold-digging ass to get back

Text him through her phone, found out where he live at
She woke up in the morning like, I never sent that
But she never told Paulie what she saw
She was running her mouth, fitting to start a war
'Cause Tony's little brother sixteen and up the wall
Robbing everything moving and breaking every law (LOOORD)
And Paulie on a rise now
Niggas that played the middle picking sides now
Plus, he heard Tony's brother trying to ride now
So, he put a check up on his head, he gotta die now

Paulie's youngest on the corner
Tony's little brother, he slippin'; yeah, he's a goner
Fucking with that Lean, he dipping one in the morning
Shots fired, niggas scatter without a warning
He strapped, too, reach and fixing to get up on 'em
The gat jam, he bang back trying to avoid 'em
Them niggas dumping, he get up running and hitting on 'em
He hit the alley, get a body he dipping on 'em
Said it's on now, try and kill 'em it's war now
Swisher in his mouth while loading his four-pound
Feeling like he dead, there ain't no remorse now
Getting high and he thinking 'bout kicking in doors now
Momma and little kids get on the floor now
Finger on the trigger, he feel that it's going down
Old ladies gotta hear that thunderstorm sound
'Cause they sad when it rain; it really gon' pour down
And it's raining like Katrina, he got thirty in his nina
Seen Paulie car, dropped thirty in his beamer
Paulie wasn't in it; when he heard it, he was steaming

Addicted to the murder, so you know that nigga fiendin'
And he want this nigga dead before Sunday hit
But youngin' tryna live on some Sunday shit
And time fly fast; it was Monday quick
And Paulie 'bout to get back on his gunplay shit
And show 'em how it's done, so he loadin' up his gun
And show this young nigga he fuck with the wrong one
Got a short temper and clutchin' the long gun
And it's on sight; he don't give a fuck if the law come

So he out here
Ridin' dirty, put down them birdies
And without fear, niggas lurking
They tryna murder heard he out there
Niggas spin 'em, they tryna hit 'em
Hitting every corner seeing niggas, but he ain't with 'em
Youngin' layin' low; he know Paulie ain't playin', though
There's money on his head and niggas is sayin' go
But youngin' he ain't scared; he cool as a fan, though
He know it's get down with that burner or end up a tag-toed
It was four in the morn', Paulie goin' home
Windshields wiping, middle of the rainstorm
And Paulie he ain't slippin'; yeah, he got that thang on
You know what he did to Tony, he won't get the same song so
When he hit the crib, he spin the block before he park it
Paulie ain't bitch at all; Paulie just cautious
But little did he know, niggas in the streets talking
And out his rearview it's like he seen a reaper walking
Nigga with a hoodie, all you hear is heaters sparking
Shot hit the window; get low, he tryna off him

Youngin' boxed him in and Paulie can see the coffin
He get to reaching, trigger squeezing, trying get him off him
Them shots ringing, youngin' squeezing clip empty
That's when Paulie rose like Derrick, put six in him
Walked down on him; he laying in a puddle
Looked him in the face, "You ain't learn from your brother, nigga?"

Meek paused after the set and gave shout outs to all of his brethren from the city, then dropped the microphone and exited the stage.

"Man, lil' homie don't fuckin' play!" Big Lou yelled excitedly, as Paulie and Trell clapped, giving props to their young homie.

After the crowd finished going wild following Meek Mill's performance, it began to thin out, but Paulie, Trell, and Big Lou partied hard with the vixens until the DJ announced the last call for alcohol.

"Boy, it's time to be up out of here. Y'all boys make sure y'all keep in touch. Y'all need to come on and get with me on some of these business ventures I'm putting down. Y'all know you can't keep ya hands in the dirt forever. Seriously, y'all get at me now," Big Lou told Paulie and Trell, then gave them dap and exited the VIP with the vixens in tow, heading out to his Rolls Royce Phantom driven by his assistant.

"That's all good, big homie, and I'll be at you, Paulie. Make sure you get with Man-Man," Trell reminded Paulie as they left behind Big Lou.

"Fa' sho," Paulie replied, stepping out the club to his waiting Audi R-8.

Just as he got behind the wheel, thunder boomed and lightening lit up the sky. Seconds later, the bottom fell out and rain drenched the once dry streets. Paulie was feeling nice. The night had put him back in contact with a lot of old friends and new money connects.

He pushed the R-8 through the pouring rain down the Philly back streets, trying to avoid the late-night patrolling Philly P.D. who would be looking to pull over anybody B.W.D.—Black While Driving. Out of habit, he reached under his seat and placed his burner on his lap, just in case any jackers were lurking at the many traffic lights and stop signs. Paulie wasn't scared; he was just cautious because he once was one of the gunners on the other side of the pistol, looking for a come up.

Entering his neighborhood, he looked at the big homes and exhaled, feeling proud for making it big in the game. As he made left on his street, lightening lit up the sky again, giving the houses a macabre look. Reaching his driveway, he mashed the gas and busted another block just in case he was being followed.

LB was across the street in the cut, waiting. When he saw Paulie pull up to his house and then drive off, he started to give chase, but decided against it. His patience paid off when Paulie came back around the block and pulled in the driveway. LB slowly pulled his hoodie over his head and got out of the car in the pouring rain.

Paulie pulled up to his garage, feeling good and not paying attention to his surroundings. He pushed the buttons on the remote for his garage door and waited while the door opened. He was feeling so good from the effects of the drinks that were flowing at the club, he was slipping, not aware of the figure that had crossed the street behind him and was creeping up the driveway looking like the Grim Reaper with a big pistol. All Paulie heard over the hard rain pounding down on the roof of the car was a gun sparking.

LB's first shot shattered the back window of Paulie's car. He ducked low and grabbed the pistol off his lap, gripping it tight. Paulie refused to see an early death, so he brought his gun up and started busting back at LB, who was letting shot after shot go.

Full of rage and adrenaline, LB emptied his clip with the notion that Paulie was a goner. His heart skipped a beat when he saw Paulie rise up out of the ride and let off a spray of shots, with six riddling his body and sending him to the wet concrete. The hard pouring rain beat the wounded LB in the face mercilessly. His hoodie had fallen back to the ground, exposing the fear in his eyes to the man now standing over him. LB frowned and squinched up his face at Paulie's last words.

"You ain't learn from your brother, nigga?" Paulie spat, then pulled the trigger of the .45.

The shot rocked his head back to the wet concrete with his brains exposed. Paulie took one good look at the young LB lying lifeless in the rain. By the time he reached the door, he heard sirens in the distance.

THE END